An
Inconvenient
ROMANCE

D1534334

AN A Regency Romance

Inconvenient

ROMANCE

CHALON LINTON

Covenant Communications, Inc.

Cover Image © Lee Avison / Trevillion Images

Cover design copyright © 2017 by Covenant Communications, Inc.

Published by Covenant Communications, Inc.
American Fork, Utah

Copyright © 2017 by Chalon Linton
All rights reserved. No part of this book may be reproduced in any format or in any medium without the
written permission of the publisher, Covenant Communications, Inc., P.O. Box 416, American Fork, UT
84003. The views expressed within this work are the sole responsibility of the author and do not neces-
sarily reflect the position of Covenant Communications, Inc., or any other entity.

This is a work of fiction. The characters, names, incidents, places, and dialogue are either products of the
author's imagination, and are not to be construed as real, or are used fictitiously.

Printed in the United States of America
First Printing: February 2017

23 22 21 20 19 18 17   10 9 8 7 6 5 4 3 2 1

978-1-52440-026-2

To those who seek the strength to forgive
and the courage to ask for forgiveness

ACKNOWLEDGMENTS

ᴄꙮ⁂ᴄꙮ

MANY THANKS TO THE COVENANT team for their dedication to making this novel shine. Special thanks to my editor, Stacey Turner, who encouraged me to push my writing and myself. She is the timeliest e-mailer I know. Thank you, Angela Piccolo, for your attention to details and overall awesomeness in creating a cover that's true to the novel. Stephanie Lacy is a marketing guru! Thank you for sharing your expertise and holding my hand on this wonderful journey.

I will forever be indebted to Andrea Blum for introducing me to Jane Austen and the wonderful world of proper gentlemen, scenic countrysides, and Darcy. To my beta readers, Jen, Kodie, Erin, Laura, and Melissa (who's been with me from the rough beginning), thanks for the honest feedback and, more importantly, your friendship. Gary Underwood, you have my devoted gratitude for sharing your talents and making me look good. A special thank-you to Stephen Tyler for his expertise and his stalwart example through the years. Janette Rallison is an example of charity. The simple act of responding to the e-mail of an eager fan and aspiring author made a world of difference to me. If you haven't read her work—do! Mountains of love to my parents for their faith in me.

Hugs and kisses to my children; they've been my cheerleaders from the beginning. Go Team Linton! All of my love to my husband, who indulged a math teacher with a sudden desire for a career change. You are a true gentleman, a devoted father, and my best friend.

Finally, believe it or not, the idea for this book came from a conversation about texting while driving. Please decide now to never text while you're behind the wheel. For the safety of all of our loved ones, the text can wait.

PROLOGUE

❧

Derbyshire, England, Summer 1811

"CHARLES CHRISTOPHER BRUMLEY! DON'T YOU dare drop that dog in the river," Leah growled as threateningly as she could. It took all of her strength to blink back her tears. She would not cry in front of him.

Charles stood laughing on the small bridge. He held the pup over the lazy river. Leah's cheeks burned bright red. She knew he was trying to push just a little harder to see if he could make her tears overflow.

"You are a horrid boy!" Leah shouted, stomping ferociously towards him. Charles placed the puppy back on the bridge and watched it scamper to the safety of the bank. Leah approached, huffing her disapproval of his game.

"Leah, you knew I wouldn't drop him," Charles defended himself. "I just wondered if he could swim."

"I knew no such thing. Admiral is only five months old and most definitely does *not* swim!" Leah turned on her heel and crossed to the bank where the puppy was sprawled on his side enjoying the warm summer day.

Charles followed her across but stopped a safe distance away. Leah sat on the grassy knoll with her back towards him and caressed the pup's soft golden fur.

"Are you going to stay mad at me all afternoon?" Charles asked with a wide smile.

"Humph!" Leah turned her nose away from him. He had pushed his antics too far today. She would not let him off so easy.

"Is this how it will be when we are married?" Charles teased as he sat down.

"What makes you think I would marry an arrogant boy like you?" Leah asked.

"You do. All those times you make me play as your prince—it always ends with a wedding."

Leah shot Charles her best look of disdain, but he simply laughed.

"Well that is too bad then. I was hoping we could settle our dispute somehow."

Leah continued to sit in silence, but her ears perked up. She slowly stroked Admiral and listened to Charles's proposal.

"A simple wager. If I win, we get to see if Admiral can swim. If you win, I must solemnly vow never to so much as sprinkle him with water."

"I'm listening," Leah said, still refusing to face him.

Charles jumped up and brushed the grass from his breeches. "A race?"

Leah smiled and scrambled to her feet. This was exactly what she had hoped for. Leah could beat him. He always insisted he let her win; however, with an official wager, Charles would have to win or admit defeat to a girl.

"Where to?" Leah asked.

"From the end of the bridge to the rose garden."

"That far?" Leah was faster than Charles, but could she maintain an advantage for that long?

Charles had already returned to the end of the bridge. "On the count of three, then." Leah walked to where he lined up. "One, two, and . . ." Charles took off running. "Three!" he shouted.

Anger boiled inside, and Leah's feet began to fly. Her skirts flapped behind her as her arms fell into a steady rhythm. Her governess would not be happy to see Leah's bonnet flapping on her back and her dark curls flying wild in the wind. But Leah had no choice. She had to catch him.

Charles made the fatal mistake of looking back. His head craned around when Leah was within an arm's length, and his face registered his shock. His feet seemed to miss a step, and he tumbled to the ground, rolling over twice in the dirt.

Leah smiled, easily leapt over his feet, and closed the final thirty yards to the garden entrance. Only once her boots crunched on the gravel path did she slow her stride. With a heaving chest, Leah turned to look back at Charles. He was sitting upright, glowering at her.

"Don't you dare say I only won because you fell," Leah said on a ragged breath. "Now admit your wager lost, and let's go enjoy some lemonade and cakes."

Charles stomped his foot in the dirt. He really thought he could take her that time. Never mind he had no intention of throwing the dog into the river. He made the bet because he thought he could win. Leah would never let him live this down.

Leah strolled back towards Charles. Her speckled brown eyes laughed, and her cheeks were once again red—this time from exertion rather than anger. Charles liked it better that way. He never meant to anger her. Although Leah was two years his junior, she was by far a better ally than an enemy, which he had learned the hard way.

Charles preferred Leah to any of the numerous male playmates his mother had forced upon him. Leah would climb trees, take a dare; she would even hook the worms when they went fishing together—not like the boys, who clung to their mothers' skirts and cowered in the nursery when a playful round of blind man's bluff was suggested.

No, Charles liked Leah and was glad his mother so frequently called on Leah's widowed aunt, Mrs. Evelyn Clem, at Astoria.

Leah offered her hand to help him up. It was bad enough to be beaten by a girl; Charles would not take her pity as well. He took hold around her wrist and pulled her into the dirt next to him. Then he stood and dusted off his breeches.

"Charles, you are the most stubborn fifteen-year-old I know. Now Miss Parks will be angry about my dress as well as my hair," Leah huffed.

"Ah, hosh posh." Charles waved her concerns away. "All you have to do is bat your eyes at your father, and you'll have a new dress by dinnertime."

Leah smirked because she knew it was true. Her father adored her. Adored her and spoiled her.

"Well, then." Leah stood and tried to tidy her appearance. It wasn't much use. "Let's see about that lemonade."

The children had settled in the nursery and were finishing their treats when Mr. Hastings appeared.

"Hello, Father." Leah curtsied quickly then ran into her father's arms.

"Ah, how are you, my darling?" Mr. Hastings asked as he spun her around then pulled her in for a close embrace.

"Oh, Father, guess what? I beat Charles in a race today!"

Mr. Hastings set Leah down and raised his eyebrows in Charles's direction. "Did you, now?"

"Yes, Father. It was so glorious. I mean, I usually beat him, but this time it was a wager, so I knew he had to try his hardest, and he did—" Leah spoke quickly and glanced at her friend. She would not let him off the hook easily. The wager was his idea after all. "Then he stumbled, and so I won!"

"That explains the dirt on your hem and the tangles in your hair." Mr. Hastings laughed as he tousled Leah's curls, adding to the disarray. "Pray tell, where was Miss Parks during this wager?"

Leah wrapped her arms around herself and watched her foot draw circles in the carpet. "Oh, I, uh, dismissed her for the day."

"Dismissed her?" Mr. Hastings eyes grew wide.

"Well, yes, Father. You know Miss Parks's mother is ill? She has been wanting to visit her for several days, and since tomorrow is her day off, I thought she might get an early start."

"And you felt within your right, as her charge, to release her from her duties?"

Charles straightened in his chair as Mr. Hastings's voice rose. One look at Leah the moment her lashes began to sweep across her eyes as delicate as butterfly wings, and Charles knew Mr. Hastings didn't stand a chance.

"But, Father." Her voice was soft. "It's her mother, and she's sick. What if . . . what if . . ." Leah's lip began to tremble, and she couldn't finish. Her point, however, had been made.

Mr. Hastings scooped her up one more time. "Yes, darling Leah. You did the right thing. Life can be too short. Miss Parks should be with her mother. I shall inquire to see if she should need more time before her return." Sighing, he gently set Leah back on her feet.

Mrs. Hastings had been sick just two years before. Her illness had been brief, and then she was gone. The pain Mr. Hastings still felt at her loss was evident on his face.

"Well, then. It looks like the two of you have the afternoon to spend together. Stay out of trouble, and please do not vex your sister." Mr. Hastings made to leave. As he reached the door, he turned back. "May I ask what your wager was for?"

Leah glanced at Charles, and his mouth turned up into a grin. He wouldn't give her the satisfaction of looking into her eyes. She turned back towards her father. "Charles wanted to throw Admiral into the river to see if he could swim." Leah fixed her hands on her hips. "Since I won, he must not even splash Admiral, or he will lose his title as a gentleman."

Mr. Hastings smiled at his defiant daughter. "Well, I do hope Admiral learns." He chuckled. "I wish to train him as my new hunting companion. Charles, when I find out if he can swim, I'll be sure to let you know." He winked at the boy, and Charles grinned wider.

Leah gasped, and Mr. Hastings made his exit.

The end of summer arrived much too quickly. Charles and Leah fished; climbed trees; harassed Leah's sister, Sarah; and kept racing until that dreadful day when Miss Parks led Leah to the drawing room.

"Oh, Charles! Hello. I did not expect to see you today." Leah plopped onto the pale-blue settee and smiled at her dear friend.

Charles looked at his mother, who nodded slightly in encouragement. "Good morning, Leah," he said. Mrs. Brumley cleared her throat loudly, and Charles corrected himself, "I mean, Miss Hastings."

Leah glanced at Charles and his mother and then turned her look of confusion to Miss Parks and Aunt Evelyn.

"Miss Hastings?" Leah laughed awkwardly. "Why, Charles, you know Sarah, being the eldest, is called Miss Hastings. I am simply Leah, or Miss Leah, if you must." She smiled.

Charles stared at his knees, and Leah's eyes searched for understanding. Mrs. Brumley sat straight backed and proper. Miss Parks's eyes darted around the room like a nervous fawn, and Aunt Evelyn continued working on her sampler. Under her breath Leah's aunt mumbled, "I don't gather that smile will last much longer." Then she spoke louder. "Dear Mr. Clem used to say, 'Spit it out, and be done with it.'"

Miss Parks jumped from her chair. "I'll check on the refreshments," she offered and slipped from the room.

Mrs. Brumley spoke. "Charles, I believe there was something you wanted to share with Miss Leah."

Charles began to squirm then abruptly stood.

Leah could be patient no longer. "Whatever is the matter? Is Rachel okay?"

Aunt Evelyn scoffed at the inquiry, and Mrs. Brumley's cheeks pressed down a pinched smile. Rather than relief, Leah felt increasingly frustrated. She stood and clutched her skirt in her fists. "Charles? What is it you have come to say?"

Charles inhaled deeply. "Miss Leah." He turned his brown eyes and fixed them on her face. "I've come to say farewell."

"Farewell?" Leah's hands released their grip, and the wrinkled fabric fell limp against her thighs.

Charles cleared his throat. "Yes, farewell." He hung his head. "I'm bound for Cambridge; I will be gone come Friday."

"Cambridge?" Leah softly repeated and dropped back onto the settee. Her brother, Ferrin, had left for university last fall, right before he was seventeen. "I thought you wouldn't go till next year." There was an emptiness in Leah's chest. This day had come too fast. She shook her head and placed a hand over her heart. She knew Charles would leave, but so soon? So unexpectedly?

"My dear," Mrs. Brumley began, her voice far too sweet to entice any reason, "Charles has been trying to tell you for some time."

Miss Parks returned at that inopportune moment with the tea tray. She began to set out the tea things, and Mrs. Brumley moved to help serve the cake.

Leah watched in silence while the hurt and anger boiled inside until it erupted in one giant burst. "You tried to tell me?" she shouted, and all three ladies' heads snapped in her direction. "Name one time, *Mr. Brumley*, that you *tried* to tell me." Leah's voice shook.

Miss Parks returned to her panicked deer demeanor, and Mrs. Brumley could scarce close her gaping jaw. Aunt Evelyn pinched her mouth together in a knowing smirk.

Leah rose and marched right up to Charles. He had grown over the summer, and the top of her head barely reached his collarbone. She jutted out her chin and stared at him, her face conveying all the pain, sorrow, and hurt she felt. "How could you? I thought we were friends, and now you're leaving?" Tears stung Leah's eyes, yet she refused to let them fall. She blinked more rapidly and choked out the words, "Charles Christopher Brumley, you are a traitor, and I never want to see you again!"

With that, Leah fled from the drawing room.

She cried to her father. Mr. Hastings hushed Leah with a gentle whisper and told her it would be all right. She didn't believe him. He had said the same thing about her mother right before she died.

The next morning, Mr. Hastings found Leah standing near the library window staring out at the rose garden. "Leah," he said, "would you like to go to Riverton Park and say farewell to the Brumleys this morning?"

"If I go, then it means he's really leaving."

"He is really leaving, whether you go or not." Leah's father laid a hand on her shoulder. "It's never good to leave things unsaid. I thought perhaps you would like to say good-bye."

Leah turned her eyes up to her father. "But I don't want to say good-bye." A single tear ran down her cheek.

They arrived at Riverton Park as the servants secured the last trunk to the traveling carriage. Mrs. Brumley spied the group and eagerly sashayed over to greet Aunt Evelyn with open arms.

Mr. Brumley gave final instructions to his steward, and Charles stepped out from the doorway. His eyes were on the dirt, and he was halfway to the carriage before Leah called his name. His head popped up, and when he saw his friend, a stifled grin filled his face. Leah couldn't resist that smile, and despite the sorrow in her heart, she returned the sentiment. Charles walked over.

"I couldn't let you remember me as a teary-eyed baby," Leah said.

"Don't worry, Miss Leah, that's not how I'll remember you," Charles replied, looking directly into her eyes. Leah felt like he could see her soul. His gaze was intent, and the burning in her heart convinced her that he knew how desperately she would miss him.

"No, of course not." Leah pulled her eyes away, her cheeks feeling warm. She looked at him from under her lashes. "You must always remember the back of my skirts so you will never forget that I can best you in a footrace."

Charles tried to twist his grin into a firm line. "I'll be home for Christmas. We'll have a rematch then," he said, finally surrendering to a smile.

Mrs. Brumley stepped into the equipage and called for Charles.

"Until then, Miss Leah." He hung his head in a stiff bow.

Leah dropped into a proper curtsy, and when she rose, Charles was climbing into the carriage. She watched the coachman turn the horses towards the lane. They began to quicken their pace, and her feet could not stand still. Leah began to run after the carriage while Mr. Hastings called for her to stop.

"Charles! Charles!" Leah yelled. Faster and faster she willed her feet forward until her legs could not keep up and she stumbled to a stop. Leah cupped her hands over her mouth and shouted, "I forgot to tell you—Admiral has learned how to swim!"

Charles's mussed brown head poked out of the side window of the carriage, and he shared one final grin before his mother yanked him back inside.

CHAPTER 1
Mr. Charles Brumley

❧

Derbyshire, England, Early Fall 1817

MY MIND SWAYED WITH THE carriage while I thought back on the day my heart changed. My chest had ached, which I first attributed to my sprint across the meadow. Then I realized that the aching didn't begin or end with my exertion. Instead, the pain was burning from the inside out and really was not painful at all.

My revelation occurred almost six years ago when I looked back at Leah, tendrils of brown hair cascading over her shoulders, free from their regular braids. In the moment I took to look at her, my feet tangled, and she leapt swiftly past me to claim victory. She reached the garden path, and in those mere seconds, in that mere glance, from her smile through her ragged breath, I knew. Though I was only fifteen, I realized I did not want to be without her—ever.

Thinking back on that day provided a mixture of happiness and nostalgic longing. I leaned my head back on the plush seat of the carriage.

"What are you smiling about?" my sister, Rachel, asked.

"I was simply wondering how you could be so excited for a simple country ball," I lied.

"Don't tease me, Charles." Rachel clasped her hands together, holding them to her chest and offering a starry-eyed gaze into the distant nowhere. "It may not compare to the grand routs in London to which you are accustomed, but you know I've dreamt of this night my entire childhood."

Rachel's dramatics made me chuckle. She dropped her hands to her lap and shot me a disparaging look.

"You found out only yesterday that you would be able to attend," I reminded her.

"Yes, well, that's because Mother didn't realize you would be home to escort me, and she was not feeling well enough to come herself." She jutted out her chin, and her soft curls bounced around on the back of her head.

"So despite the teasing, you *are* grateful I'm here?" I asked with a grin and raised eyebrows. She allowed her eyes to dart towards me for a quick second then resumed her defiant posture. "Otherwise, all of your childhood dreams would have come to naught. And at the tender age of fifteen, it would have been such a pity." I looked at her with mock solemnity. "And now you are in my debt, seeing as how I rode into town on my white stallion just in time to take you to the ball."

Rachel pressed her lips together, exhaled through her nose, and said, "Your horse is brown, Charles. And I am not a character from the Brothers Grimm. But, yes, I suppose I can endure your incorrigible behavior and even," she paused, raising her chin a little higher, "acknowledge that I am grateful."

"Well, well, Rachel, perhaps you are ready to be whisked around the dance floor." I had come as a favor to Rachel, but I had also come as a favor to myself. It had been far too long since I'd been home.

At Cambridge, I had immersed myself in school, only returning home for Christmas holiday. There were frequent thoughts of Leah and our days spent in the sun. I'd memorized every freckle on her face and every errant curl on her head. The memories brought comfort when I was studying for an especially hard exam or when the wind in the trees taunted me to come run in the clean air. The pains of homesickness never hit, yet often there was a nagging pain in my chest—right over my heart—and I knew I felt sick for her.

Leah should, and I most ardently hoped *would*, be in attendance tonight. Surprising Rachel had been enjoyable, but I longed to see Leah's face when I asked her to dance.

The carriage stopped then lurched again as we continued forward, awaiting our turn to disembark.

Rachel's eyes were wide, and she wrung her gloved hands in her lap. My lips curved as I observed her youthful innocence, at the same time acknowledging the havoc my nerves were inflicting on me. My stomach tightened, and in response I flexed my muscles, hoping to control the knots that were forming.

We finally pulled to a complete stop in front of the entrance and waited for the footman to lower the step. After a deep breath, I exited and turned back to offer a hand to Rachel. She gathered her skirts and gave me a weak smile. Looking at her, I wondered what I had to fear. This was far from the first ball I had attended, and a simple country gathering could in no way compete with the grand crush of London. But neither could the cold and distant ton compare to the eager company flooding into the Assembly Hall.

Yet it was not the ball that caused this uneasiness to engulf me. Rather it was the prospective company. Though I had no right to think of Leah as mine, I did. We had seen each other sporadically over the past six years—when I would return for holiday or, most recently, when I returned to bury my father. But I had thought of her every day. From my moment of enlightenment on that summer afternoon, Leah had consumed my spare thoughts, and to be honest, she consumed more than that. I thought of her when I studied poetry and when I walked the banks of the Thames. I thought of her when I attended the theater, remembering the make-believe stories we used to enact on the bluff near her home. I thought of her always—waiting, anticipating the time when I could confess all the feelings of my heart and ask her to be mine.

Rachel tugged on my arm, bringing my attention back to her. The doors of the Assembly Hall taunted me. The volume of the gathering crowd intensified and washed like a wave through the mass of attendees.

My last trip home had been ten months ago. As soon as Father's funeral had concluded, I left. I could not stomach the gossip, the stares, the sympathy, nor the pain. But Mother had written once again, urging me to return and tend to the estate, and my excuses had run thin.

Mother had also informed me that she was unwell and that Rachel, my only sibling, desperately wanted to attend this, her first ball. It was not the first time Mother had asked me to come home, but something in this particular letter urged me forward. Perhaps the mention of a certain handsome captain who seemed set on courting Leah. Mother did not mince words. I rode home immediately.

Rachel stood on her tiptoes and whispered near my ear. "See, they are all eager to see you."

"Don't be ridiculous," I scolded her, flexing my arm to play with her further. "They are merely in awe of your beauty, for you look very lovely tonight."

Rachel's cheeks burned bright, and she looked at her feet as we entered the hall.

The happy murmur of voices quickly returned to a lull, and my eyes scanned the exterior walls, searching for the face that filled my dreams.

"Mr. Brumley!" a deep voice boomed. My attention turned from the borders of the room to focus on Mr. Harrison, who was suddenly much too close.

Rachel tugged again on my arm. "Oh, Charles, there is Gwendolyn. She looks divine! May I please go join her?"

"Yes, if you promise to save me the first dance."

Rachel agreed and scampered away, and I resigned myself to limit my search for Leah to what I could see over Mr. Harrison's shoulder.

The man provided a detailed update on the state of Mrs. Harrison's health, complete with an in-depth description of Dr. Hutchins's most recent diagnosis.

Thankfully, the musicians took their seats and the next dance was called. After extricating myself from Mr. Harrison, I turned to retrieve Rachel. I pushed through the crowd, and while everything was familiar, it was crushing. Mothers seeking introductions for their daughters, old friends wanting to reacquaint, and I had already lost sight of my sister, the sole reason I had come—or so I claimed. In my continuous search for Rachel, I made excuses all around and pushed through the crowd.

After wedging myself through a boisterous group of women, I emerged to find a rainbow. Laughing—and somehow I knew it was at me—was Leah.

A smile, reserved for a long time, erupted, and I immediately crossed to her. My initial instinct was to sweep her into a hug, as I had my sister when I had arrived home the day before. It seemed the natural thing to do. But my arms stiffened at my side, and instead of an embrace, I bowed.

Leah matched my smile and curtsied in return.

To see those eyes—her bewitching brown eyes smiling back at me—I lived that blessed epiphany all over again.

I had imagined this moment so many times, played it out in my head—how natural the conversation would flow, like all those years ago. I opened my mouth, waiting for the words to form.

"Miss Leah, I believe you have promised me this dance."

Only the words weren't mine.

A stranger, an officer in uniform, extended his hand, and with a slight blush, Leah placed her gloved fingers in his.

Leah bowed her head towards me again. "Excuse me, Mr. Brumley," she said with a smile and walked to the dance floor.

"I have the worst timing ever," I whispered under my breath. My heart felt like a horse had trampled every pulsing vein. I watched the blond soldier smile at Leah, and she coyly returned his gaze.

Rachel's sudden appearance at my side ended my subjugation. I had promised my sister a dance.

CHAPTER 2
Miss Leah Hastings

❧ ❧ ❧

I HAD BEEN LOOKING FORWARD to the ball at the Assembly Hall for some time. Never in my dreams, or at least my recent ones, did I imagine Charles would be in attendance.

I had heard that Mrs. Brumley was unwell. Perhaps it was more serious than I had been led to believe. Aunt Evelyn had called at Riverton Park yesterday. Surely she would have mentioned if Mrs. Brumley was on her deathbed, for it would take such an extreme circumstance to bring Charles back to Derbyshire.

He hadn't been home since his father's sudden passing nearly ten months ago, and even then I had only spoken with him long enough to offer my condolences. I had wanted to offer more, but he was cold and distant. When his father died, so did Charles's carefree innocence. He wouldn't humor me in my attempts to lighten the moment or smile when I referenced some prank we had pulled years ago. His brown eyes had pulled back into their depths and turned cold; he returned to Town as soon as he was able, leaving the affairs of the estate to his father's former steward.

Now as he crossed towards me, I recognized all that was familiar, and as I slowly searched him a second time, I took in all that had changed. The boyish fullness of his cheeks had been replaced with a firm, confident jaw. He held his shoulders back with an air of superiority, one that seemed to fit the precise cut of his jacket. He was dashing to be sure, and while I was not surprised, I felt relieved to find my assessment of him to be so complimentary. The sun was back in his eyes. Gone were the shadows that had stolen his smile, and I knew they would not return tonight because he was smiling at me. Wide and broad and full of a warmth I recognized.

What could be the cause of Charles's evolution? Perhaps he had returned to share news. Could he be engaged? My heart jumped at the thought before I remembered I should not care if he were engaged. He was simply a friend.

I dismissed my folly and returned Charles's smile with one of my own.

He had barely reached me when the musicians completed tuning their instruments and signaled the beginning of the dance. Captain Wilkins came to claim my hand.

Captain Wilkins was the one I had dressed so carefully for tonight. I had wanted him to notice me, to gain some security of his affections. He had called several times at Astoria, but inside the drawing room with my sister and Aunt Evelyn, Captain Wilkins became quiet.

Sarah teased that he would make the perfect husband because my tongue would compensate for the both of us. She didn't know him as I did. Captain Wilkins was soft-spoken, but he was also kind and attentive and very well read. It also didn't hurt that he was an extremely handsome gentleman. His tan skin and golden hair testified of his love for the outdoors—as did his strong, square shoulders and well-tailored uniform.

Captain Wilkins and I had met during my short season in London. He had left for his station with a promise to call at Astoria when leave was granted. He had kept that promise and arrived in Derbyshire four days ago.

His long legs led me around the dance floor, and he showered me with attention and praise beyond what I deserved, but his admiration was nonetheless appreciated. I would need to thank my maid, Gerty, for the extra attention she paid to my hair this evening. Many eyes and whispers were directed towards us.

"You look lovely tonight," Captain Wilkins said. His lips turned into a soft smile, and I saw the corner of his mouth twitch, threatening to turn into a full grin.

"Thank you." I wondered why he kept his enthusiasm under such tight control. I wanted him to unleash, to show himself wholly, to share the secret behind his twinkling blue eyes.

The music dictated our steps, turning us past Charles and Rachel. I tried to catch Charles's attention, to remind him of the many times I made him practice dancing with me, preparing for a night such as this. Mr. Brumley remained focused on his sister, and my eyes returned to my partner.

The dance ended, and Captain Wilkins led me from the floor. The air hung heavy, and although he now held my arm, my skin was warm through my gloves. Heat resonated where our hands had touched.

"Would you care to dance another?" Captain Wilkins asked with such a direct stare that a burning began in my chest and crept up through my neck. He was so very handsome, and the cool blue of his eyes reminded me of an oasis—a reprieve for which I had been searching a long time.

He was waiting for my answer. It was too hot. My body could not carry me through another dance—at least not without cooling off first. "I think I shall step onto the terrace for some fresh air," I said, and Captain Wilkins's disappointment was immediately obvious. "Could I perhaps postpone your invitation until the waltz?" I asked. The waltz was a more intimate dance, and he accepted my suggestion with a suppressed smile and nod of his head.

"I'll get some punch," he said and walked towards the refreshments.

A waltz with Captain Wilkins would allow me to visit that oasis in rhythm to the swaying music, or perhaps it was simply the first thought that popped into my head.

I needed to breathe something cooler than the oppressive heat of the ballroom.

On the terrace, I leaned against the banister, listening to the giggles and declarations of love whispered from a bench tucked away in the shadows. I smiled and tried to conjure a breeze by fanning myself with my hand.

"Would this help?" Charles walked up beside me and proceeded to flap both of his hands near my face.

"Oh, stop!" I laughed and swatted his arm.

His dark eyes grew large in mocked offense; then his lips turned into a grin. We stood there, both of us watching the other, waiting for something to snap. Despite my many questions for Charles, he was the one who left. I would not be the first to begin.

An awkward silence hung in the stagnant air between us.

Finally, Charles cleared his throat. "How are you, Miss Leah?"

My face softened, and the burning in my chest subsided. "I am well, Mr. Brumley. What brings you home?"

"Rachel wanted to dance," he said simply.

"You are determined to be a good brother, then?"

He opened his mouth then closed it again and simply said, "I am."

The silence settled comfortably after letting those first words slide out into the night. Charles leaned his elbows on the railing and clasped his hands.

"Mother had not mentioned any regiments in Paddington," he said.

"There are none."

"And the gentleman you were dancing with?"

"An acquaintance from London," I said, feeling no need to explain to Charles how deep or shallow that acquaintance was.

As expected, he pressed for more. "And he's stationed nearby?"

"No, his unit is in Oxfordshire. Captain Wilkins is on leave."

"On leave? And he chose to come here?"

"Yes. Would you like to see his orders?" I asked curtly.

"No, that won't be necessary," he said casually. His lack of contrition stirred my anger.

"It may seem unfathomable to you, Mr. Brumley, but some people do prefer the country, Derbyshire, in fact, to anywhere else. It really is a delightful place if you recall."

Charles shrugged. "It's adequate."

"Adequate!" My mouth dropped open, and I glared at him. He was obviously as obstinate as ever. Some things did not change.

"Yes, adequate. I don't think Derbyshire itself is what holds the enticement." He looked directly at me, studying my face and gaping jaw. "I think what is *in* Derbyshire holds the enticement."

I pursed my lips together to keep my frustration from escaping my mouth in words I would want to take back later. After a few calming breaths, I replied, "Then I wonder why you stayed away so long."

"Leah." Charles stood straight, and his face softened, causing my chest to hurt in an entirely different way.

"If you'll excuse me, Mr. Brumley." I offered a small curtsy. "The waltz is about to begin, and Captain Wilkins is expecting me."

The caustic air of the ballroom enveloped me as I stepped back inside and left Charles standing alone.

CHAPTER 3
Mr. Charles Brumley

I RUBBED MY HAND ACROSS my face. She wanted to know why I had stayed away. The trouble was I didn't know myself. No, that wasn't entirely true. I hadn't come back, and the reason was irrevocably linked to the cause for which I had left in the first place: Leah.

When I left for Cambridge, I immersed myself in school, and when I returned home, Leah and I would become reacquainted only to have to say good-bye again. The good-byes became harder and harder, but I had to return to my studies.

After receiving my degree, I found freedom. Freedom to live the life I wanted. The entire world had been opened to me through my studies of mathematics, the sciences, music, classic literature, and—my favorite— philosophy. I longed to grow and expand into so much more than I had in my twenty-one years.

When I returned home, Leah and I slipped back into the familiar, but this time there was something more—expectations.

Father wanted me to begin taking over the business of the estate. He insisted I call on all of the tenants, that I join him in meetings with his steward, and that I begin maintaining the ledgers.

Mother pushed for prestige. She wanted me to become involved in Parliament and had the audacity to suggest I approach my distant cousin and appeal for his seat in the House of Commons. Neighbors presumed expertise to my plans and future. It seemed everyone had an opinion about my life. They pressed again and again. It was too crushing, and I would not yield. Instead, I fled.

My father died of illness three months later. I returned home for the service, and suddenly everything I didn't want—and wasn't ready for— was pushed upon me. So I pushed right back. I passed off the duties at

Riverton Park and returned to Town. I had to figure out what I wanted from life.

My college acquaintances avoided me because I was brooding and irritable. And the lonely nights in London drove me into a deep depression. I yearned for my carefree childhood days, though I knew they would not return. I kept grasping for something that would always be out of reach.

Then Mother's last letter arrived, the one where she mentioned Rachel's first ball and the expected arrival of a certain captain. Suddenly the fog cleared. Jealousy hit me with a gigantic wallop, and I knew that the thing I coveted from my youth was a feeling, a sentiment, an emotion all wrapped into a beautiful package named Leah Hastings.

My course was determined.

I rode home immediately to discover that Captain Wilkins had arrived two days prior. I'd always had rotten timing. Now they were dancing, holding on to each other, united as one with the music. Jealousy raged in my breast, and I knew it was time to fight for my dream.

I returned to the ballroom and located Rachel engaged in a lively conversation with Miss Sarah Hastings and Mrs. Clem. Realizing Rachel was managing well, I most definitely did *not* turn my eyes to the dance floor. I did not want to see him and her floating across the floor, gazing whimsically at each other.

I had been the one to practice those steps with her over and over when the rain drove us to play inside and she had begged me to teach her how to dance. It should be me leading her around the floor, holding her in my arms, staring into her eyes . . . but it wasn't.

The refreshments would provide a distraction. I walked across the room and poured myself a drink. The cool punch was a reprieve from the stifling air, but it did nothing to cool the simmering inside. Intrigue pulled my gaze back to the dance floor. My eyes scanned the waves of dancers, looking for a blond soldier and a dark-haired beauty.

My search failed, and instead Mrs. Ansley stepped into view.

"Mr. Brumley," she said enthusiastically and fell into a curtsy. "I did not realize we would be graced with your presence this evening."

"It was a surprise to me as well," I managed to say without choking on my punch.

She turned to stand beside me and followed my eyes to the dance floor. "Is there something or *someone* in particular that has brought you home?"

I ignored her.

"My dear Catherine is looking charming tonight, is she not?" She motioned with her pointy chin to her daughter, who was socializing not far away.

"She is looking well, Mrs. Ansley." The last bars of the waltz faded from the instruments. "If you will excuse me." I took one step then looked back as she quietly harrumphed her disapproval. "Oh, and, Mrs. Ansley— Rachel. Rachel is the reason I'm here tonight." Let her have no reason to flap her tongue and contrive another purpose for my return. I had come for Rachel, and as far as the other reason, I was still contemplating my plan of attack.

Captain Wilkins's blond head caught my eye, and I followed as he led Leah towards her sister and mine. I walked up as Leah was introducing Rachel to the tall stranger.

"Oh!" Leah seemed startled by my sudden appearance. "And may I introduce Mr. Charles Brumley, Miss Brumley's brother."

Captain Wilkins bowed cordially, and I did the same. Leah looked at Sarah, who stood with a mischievous gleam in her eye. The moment stretched on long and quiet. Leah parted her lips to speak, but I cut her off.

"Miss Leah, I believe I have this next dance?" It was a lie, and her eyes widened at my bold assertion. She speared me with a look I'd seen many times when we were younger. My actions were often determined by her reactions. I usually loved that startled expression, the one that lit her entire face. Tonight it scared me. I extended my hand and waited.

Slowly she exhaled and placed her fingers in mine. My lips twitched, wanting to erupt into a broad smile, which I knew better than to reveal.

Captain Wilkins's voice interrupted my reverie. "It would be a shame for your sister to miss out on an opportunity to dance the quadrille. With your permission, Mr. Brumley, may I request her hand for this dance?"

Rachel looked at me with wide, eager eyes. Evidently everyone wanted to dance with Captain Wilkins. I begrudgingly acquiesced, and they followed Leah and me to the floor.

Captain Wilkins and Rachel stopped and took up position near us. Right before the music began, I tugged Leah's hand and pulled her away from the captain and his dashing good looks.

"What was that for, Mr. Brumley?" Leah whispered.

"There was need for another couple at this end of the room," I said.

She scoffed and rolled her eyes at my answer.

The music began, and we moved together. Leah's familiar smell filled my senses—a warm, outdoor breeze mixed with something new . . . lavender? We stepped around another couple then joined again. Her long, slender fingers fit naturally in mine. I led her through the steps until the dance required us to separate again.

Sometimes as we joined together, she appeared as if she was about to share some great joke, but then the brightness would retreat and her eyes would turn distant. Eventually she did speak.

"It's been a while since we have shared a dance, Mr. Brumley," she said coolly.

"I don't think you have ever shared a dance with Mr. Brumley, only Charles." I hoped to draw another smile. Instead, I saw her glance to the far end of the room. My stomach clenched, and I pulled her closer to my side. "You've moved on without me," I whispered.

Her eyes snapped back to mine, and fury burned within. "You left!" she huffed. "Was I supposed to wallow? To wait indefinitely for your return?"

We separated again and watched another couple turn between us. Finally, we rejoined in the center.

"There were some things I had to figure out," I said.

Leah froze, and I stopped with her as the music and movement continued around us.

"And you would not allow me to help? You refused to share what was going on. You fled. Without a word. Without an explanation." Leah inhaled sharply. Lowering her voice, she spoke again. "I tried to talk to you, Charles; I tried to tell you—" Her voice caught, and I saw the forlorn pleading in her eyes. "I was without hope."

"It didn't take you long to find it again, I see." The words left my mouth before I could reel them back.

Leah's face burned red, and she blinked rapidly to keep the tears in her eyes. "That's not fair, Charles. You're the one who left. You moved on long before I did."

She turned her back and walked away from me—again.

CHAPTER 4
Miss Leah Hastings

CHARLES AND I HAD DANCED many times before, but those dances felt like child's play compared to Charles's steps just now. They were sure and purposeful, his hands firm and strong, gripping me with an intense longing that, despite the torrid heat, sent goose pimples racing up my arms. It was vastly different than my reaction to Captain Wilkins, and I struggled to account for it.

Charles broached a subject that I had closed up in my heart. I had shut away the questions and the hurt and moved forward. Then, suddenly, he showed up demanding explanations. It was too much.

I've moved on without him? What nerve! I moved on because he left me no choice in the matter. I had waited for him for years. Ever since he left for school, I had been stalwart and faithful. Our reunions were short, yet they were simple and enjoyable, a little glimpse into what the future could hold. But after Cambridge, something changed. And with that something, everything.

I didn't want our differences to ruin Rachel's night, but I could not stand there and be scrutinized for something that was *his* doing. So I walked away. It was, after all, what Charles had taught me to do.

The veranda offered an easy escape, and I found that the bench hidden in the darkness had been abandoned. I sat and braced my arms on either side against the cool stone. My breath was ragged and rushed, angry and confused. Bars of music streamed through the open door. When I leaned my head back against the wall, the pins in my hair pressed painfully into my skull. It was too much effort to sit like an elegant lady, so I stood and walked to the banister.

What had caused Charles to leave, and what had brought him home? Why couldn't I bar this part of my heart? I thought I had barricaded him far away, unable to hurt me again. But the flaw in my plan was that I never considered he would return.

I was ready to leave. I had looked forward to the night for quite some time, and considering that I had danced with Captain Wilkins and he had called me beautiful, my purpose for the evening was fulfilled. Sarah had come reluctantly anyhow. Her beau, Mr. Dashel, was in Town, and she would soon return there to accept his proposal of marriage. She had come tonight only to pacify me.

In the doorway, I stood on my tiptoes to survey the ballroom. Where had my sister and aunt disappeared? Instead of my family, I saw Mrs. Ansley. Her lips were pinched tight, along with her brows, and when we made eye contact, she scorched me with a glare that left my throat dry. My head jerked with a start, and I opened my eyes wide, unsure what could have provoked her wrath.

My eyes quickly turned back to the dance floor. Mr. Brumley and Rachel were progressing through the line and were now a few yards away. I smiled for a moment, watching Rachel's youthful innocence light up her face. Suddenly Mr. Brumley spun into view, caught my eye, and winked at me. Audacious man!

I glared back at him until I saw Mrs. Ansley set on a very determined course towards me. While Mrs. Ansley had been a familiar acquaintance of my late mother, I had never felt comfortable in her presence. The truth was she frightened me. With her pomp, her sharp tongue, and the feathers sticking out of her hair, she reminded me of the geese my father used to keep near the fishing pond—beautiful from a distance, but up close they were spiteful creatures. The last thing I wanted was a confrontation with an ornery waterfowl.

I decided to circle the room to locate Sarah. A girl I recognized from the village waved hello, and I nodded back.

"Miss Leah." Mrs. Ansley lingered on the *S* then spit out the rest of my name.

Drat. The woman caught me. I steeled my reserve, squared my shoulders, and turned around slowly. "Mrs. Ansley," I began, "it's lovely to see you this evening."

"Is it?" she sneered.

"Where is Catherine? Dancing?" I hoped to take control of the conversation.

"She is," Mrs. Ansley snipped. "Mr. Moore has the honor of this dance."

"Lovely," I said.

"Miss Leah, do not think you can hide your intentions from me." Intentions? I could not hide my shock. What was the woman talking about? Mrs. Ansley continued. "Your mother was a dear friend of mine; however, that does not mean I will sit idly by and watch you cavort and connive away my daughter's future. Mr. Brumley has returned to seek her hand, and you, with your"—she flipped her fingers around in front of me from my bodice to my brow—"finery, does not change that."

Shock stilled the breath in my lungs.

"I trust you understand my meaning and will stop this charade immediately." Mrs. Ansley whipped out her fan and turned her pointy chin towards the dance floor.

Angry heat pulsed through me. How dare she attempt to dictate my actions? How dare she insinuate that my intentions were less than honorable, that my goal was to snare an unsuspecting husband. Mr. Brumley no less!

"Do I make myself clear?" She clicked off each word with her mock tone of authority.

"Perfectly." My hands curled into fists at my side. What nerve! In that moment, I realized that the musicians were playing the last refrains of the song. I looked towards the floor, where Catherine was ignoring Mr. Moore as her eyes scanned the periphery of the room.

Mr. Brumley offered a feigned smile to Rachel, put her arm in his, and began to lead her in my direction. Catherine allowed Mr. Moore to escort her off the floor; they too were heading our way.

"Leah, you look lovely tonight," Catherine gushed after Mr. Moore excused himself. Catherine's eyes were bright and happy. "Are you here with your family?" Her mother scoffed and rolled her eyes. The difference between mother and daughter was uncanny.

My fingers uncurled, and I answered, "Unfortunately, Ferrin and Father could not attend. Sarah and my dear aunt came with me this evening." Catherine's smile seemed to falter, but I did not have time to question her further, for Charles had released Rachel to visit with a friend and was now quickly approaching.

"Excuse me, Miss Ansley. Mrs. Ansley." I offered a shallow curtsey to each in turn and closed the few steps between Charles and myself. Charles owed me one. Actually, he owed me a lot more, but right now he could give Mrs. Ansley a proper set down. Charles could have a temporary respite in order to remind Mrs. Ansley that her threats did not determine my actions.

His deep eyes searched my face, asking wordlessly what I wanted from him. I trusted he would figure it out. It took him a moment, standing in a stupid shock, until realization dawned and he asked me to dance.

"With pleasure," I proclaimed much louder than necessary.

Mr. Brumley grasped my hand in his and gave my fingers a gentle squeeze as he led me to the floor. "Does this mean I'm forgiven?" he asked.

"Not in the least," I said and turned around to see Mrs. Ansley's jaw hanging open. A smile and small tilt of my head caused her mouth to snap shut.

My behavior was unbecoming, and it was wrong to involve Charles in my scheme—for Mrs. Ansley had a very loose tongue—but the satisfaction of the moment supplied me with enough fortitude to survive the rebuke I would no doubt receive from Sarah.

"Are you well?" Mr. Brumley whispered as he guided me into place. His eyes were full of concern. "You have no obligation to dance with me."

I let out a stifled laugh. "Mr. Brumley, you have changed." The thought was sobering, and my head tilted to take in the familiar depth behind his searching gaze.

"Forgive me?" he asked tentatively, unsure if the change was a positive one.

His uncertainty was amusing. "Not too many years ago, the only concern you would have expressed is that someone else had vexed me before you had the chance."

He lowered his head and twisted his lips into a grin. Then he stood at his full height and looked at me once more. "I only meant to verify that you truly wanted to share this dance with me. I wouldn't want to steal you away from another gentleman. Perhaps you were waiting for an alternate invitation?" His warmth disappeared with his last question.

"Mr. Brumley, your request was ideal in every way," I assured him. The music began, and with my hand in Charles's, we stepped into the rhythm of the song.

CHAPTER 5
Mr. Charles Brumley

SITTING ON THE EDGE OF my bed, I let my valet pull the boots from my feet. Then I dismissed him so I could wallow alone.

Pacing the length of my room did nothing to ease the tumult I felt. I ran my fingers through my hair, willing my head to come up with some reason, some rational explanation I could share with Leah to tell her why I had been away.

I could tell her that after my father passed I was broken. I did not feel worthy of the expectations that suddenly fell to me. Riverton Park, the tenants, the management—it was all too much, so I left the responsibility in the capable hands of Father's steward. But that explanation held only a sliver of truth.

I had rejected Leah before that dreadful day. Prior to my father's death, expectations were made known to me that I could not fulfill. How could I tell her it was *her* expectations that had pushed me away? How could it be that the same expectations I ran from were the ones that brought me home? It was all her fault, and I had no clue what to do about it.

The following morning, I dismounted and handed my horse to the groom at Astoria.

Jensen met me at the door. "Mr. Brumley, it has been a long time," the old butler said as he took my hat and gloves.

"Indeed it has. Too long." Not much had changed in my time away. The stairs to the right of the entrance were lined with Hastings family portraits. An oversized chandelier hung in the center of the hall. It had been a wedding gift from a distant royal relation, and Leah's mother wanted it hung for all to see. Leah told me she personally thought it was much better suited to the dinning room, and her father agreed. But after her mother's death, it was decided that the chandelier should remain in the hall as a tribute to Mrs. Hastings.

Astoria was not as large as Riverton Park; however, it was much older and had passed through generations with pride. Though the property was not as grand, it had a reverent, dignified ambiance. Leah had always been proud of her home. I reflected on the many happy hours spent within these walls.

Jensen stood patiently waiting for me to finish my recollections.

"I was hoping to call on Miss Leah," I told him.

"Ah, her *second* caller of the day." He raised one bushy eyebrow.

"Second?" It was barely noon on the morning after a ball! I was pushing propriety to arrive so early. Who could have called first?

In the next second, I knew. Laughter rang out from the drawing room. Laughter I recognized as Leah's.

Jensen looked at me as if I were a sodden kitten. I shook off his pity. "Will you announce me, or shall I do it myself?" I started towards the offending laughter.

"Yes, sir." Jensen smirked as he quickened his step and beat me to the room. He tapped lightly, pushed the door farther ajar, and stated my name.

The laughter ceased abruptly, and I stepped inside. The women stood—Miss Leah, Miss Hastings, and Mrs. Clem. Captain Wilkins stayed seated on the pale-blue settee. I gave my acknowledgment, and the ladies reclaimed their seats.

Mrs. Clem spoke. "Mr. Brumley, how good it is to see you. How long has it been since you were last at Riverton Park?"

Before I could respond, Leah did. "Ten months this coming week." She blinked once before lowering her eyes to her hands clasped in her lap.

While her comment was meant to shame me, it had the opposite effect. It gave me hope, a reason to fight. She had known, with acute precision, when I was last at home. Leah kept track. She kept track of me, and that must mean that somewhere deep down she still cared.

I chose the armchair next to Mrs. Clem. She had always been tolerant of me. I was determined to wait out Captain Wilkins, both today and in the future. His interest in Leah was obvious. Surely they did not have an understanding? She would have mentioned it last night. To avoid Leah's contemptuous glare, I addressed her sister. "Miss Hastings, my mother told me you will be returning to London. I understand that Mr. Dashel will soon be a very happy man."

"Perhaps. We will see." Miss Hastings's cheeks reddened slightly, and she tried to deflect the conversation. "I will be staying with my aunt and uncle for the holiday."

"Your mother's brother? Mr. Barnes?" I asked, and Sarah confirmed with a nod. "We were introduced when he was here at Astoria. A delightful man." It was only fair that Captain Wilkins knew he was dealing with an old family friend.

Leah rolled her eyes.

Ignoring her, I continued. "And you, Captain Wilkins, what might your future hold?" No point in beating around the bush.

"I report back to my unit in Oxfordshire come Monday. But hopefully I shall be returning very soon to Derbyshire." The man didn't miss a beat. He slowly moved his eyes to Leah, and the corner of his mouth turned up into a smile. The good captain had just declared war!

Leah fought the blush creeping into her cheeks. She raised her chin, and I could see the challenge in her eyes. "And what might your plans be, Mr. Brumley? Surely you're not planning on staying long." She tilted her head and offered a coy smile. "After all, it seems Town is more suited to your taste than the country."

"And so it begins," Mrs. Clem said under her breath. I looked at her, but she feigned nonchalance and clipped an excess string from her embroidery.

Turning back and staring at Leah, I answered, "There you would be incorrect. I believe the country can provide far better for my wants . . . and needs."

Leah's shoe wagged beneath the hem of her dress. She always twitched her foot when she was uncomfortable. It was her unique way of dissipating her nerves without revealing them. The fluttering of her hemline warmed my heart and bolstered my courage.

Mrs. Clem shifted and produced an obvious fake cough. "Shall I ring for tea?" She directed a mischievous smile at Sarah.

I stood. "Not for me, thank you. I simply wanted to offer a quick hello. We will have plenty of opportunities to renew our acquaintance." I stepped towards the door. "Godspeed, Captain Wilkins," I said.

And I meant it.

CHAPTER 6
Miss Leah Hastings

❦

ARROGANT, SELF-RIGHTEOUS, GLOATING BOY! THAT was what I remembered Charles to be, and he confirmed every sentiment when he came to call yesterday.

Sarah and I had it all arranged. Captain Wilkins would call, and Aunt Evelyn would allow us to walk in the gardens where she could supervise from the library window. It would give us privacy, and provide Captain Wilkins an opportunity to declare himself.

Then Charles showed up and ruined everything! He always did.

After Charles excused himself, Captain Wilkins followed. He would not return until mid-October and then only so long as the roads remained passable. I thought the separation might encourage him to propose before he left, but considering that he had not met with Father to ask for my hand—I had cajoled that tidbit from Jensen—I would not become engaged this week.

Wandering alone through the gardens, my mind refused to focus on the simplicity of the changing seasons. The peaceful summer would soon subside to a blustering autumn, and my shawl would not be adequate much longer. I pulled the soft wool tighter around my shoulders and continued towards the bridge, relishing my many memories of playing here with Charles.

Was Charles really staying? No. I could not let my mind, or my heart, consider the possibility. Mrs. Ansley would be pleased, and perhaps she could press her poor daughter upon Mr. Brumley. It would serve him right to have her as a mother-in-law. The wicked thought brought a smile to my face.

While Mrs. Ansley had insisted that just such an arrangement was the reason for Charles's return, I did not believe her. Still, I could not account for his sudden reappearance. To be gone entirely from home with not so much as a word and then return just as suddenly. His presence was shrouded in a mystery I could not put far from my mind. In order to keep my thoughts in any semblance of order, I had to remind myself that Charles left *me* when he left Derbyshire. Now it was time to move on. The mantra had tucked him away into the furthest recess of my heart, and I constantly repeated it in order to keep any wandering sentiment locked up tight.

Unavoidably, when I thought the strings were securely drawn, the question would always return—what brought him home? It would be two more days before I could question him further.

Upon returning from my afternoon walk with Admiral, I found Aunt Evelyn and Sarah engaged with company in the drawing room. It was Mr. Brumley.

He rose upon my entrance. "Miss Leah." His voice was welcoming like the soft breeze I had left outdoors, and I hated the comfort I felt in hearing it. In his eyes lingered a vague memory of what we had once shared.

I quickly pushed it away and greeted him with a neutral expression.

"Mr. Brumley brought a bouquet of . . . something or other." Sarah waved a dismissive hand towards a cluster of small purple flowers on the table between two armchairs.

"Forget-me-nots?" I asked. They were my favorite flower.

Charles tipped his head and grinned his familiar grin.

The irony was laughable. Had he really listened all those days ago? No, I would not think on it!

Still, I had my manners. "Thank you," I said and sat across the room from him.

There was an awkward silence until Aunt Evelyn called for tea. After we had all been served, I stood at the window and gazed at the old oak tree outside. The branches danced about in the breeze. Sometimes the gusts were subtle and other times violent, but the gray arms of the oak stretched towards heaven, inevitably swayed by wind, never able to reach the sky they struggled to grab a hold of.

Mr. Brumley stepped up beside me. "I have many fond memories of climbing that tree."

"Have you changed that much, Char—" I cleared my throat. "Excuse me. Mr. Brumley?"

"You know, every time you call me that, I look around for my late father." His eyes turned sad for a moment. He shook it off and leaned towards me. "I really do wish you'd call me Charles, as you have before."

My neck felt suddenly warm, and I could not account for it. I had called him Charles far more often than Mr. Brumley. In fact, when I thought about him, Charles was the name that came to mind. "We have grown up, Mr. Brumley. But perhaps in time—if you truly are planning on staying for a while."

"I am." His earnest answer pricked my heart, and for some reason I believed him.

Ferrin burst through the door, and Charles and I spun around at the commotion.

"Brumley!" Ferrin exclaimed. "How are you?"

Charles stepped forward and greeted my elder brother with a vigorous handshake. Ferrin was twenty-seven. He and I looked more like Father, and while I thought my natural dark curls were one of my best features, Ferrin tried to tame his wavy locks. Ferrin also had Father's sharp nose, and though mine was not so pronounced, my angular chin and cheekbones could not compare to Sarah's femininity. Sarah was two years older than my twenty years. She had inherited my mother's soft features: golden hair, golden skin, and gentle curves in her face.

"Sarah told me you were at the Assembly Hall. I had some business to attend to, but had I known you would be there, I would have postponed." Ferrin stepped back and shared his easy smile.

"I shall remain at Riverton Park until some things are resolved," Charles said.

"Anything of concern?" Ferrin asked.

"Not at all." Charles's eyes moved to mine. He shifted his stance and looked at Ferrin once more. "You will have to come shooting. The pheasants at Riverton Park have become far too complacent."

"Agreed! Father asked me to check some renovations. Care to join me?"

"No, thank you. I should be going. Mother planned for an early supper tonight."

"Then I shall see you out," Ferrin said.

Mr. Brumley bowed to each of us in turn and followed Ferrin into the hall.

The air released from my lungs, and I turned back to the window. It seemed so easy for him to waltz back into our lives as if he never left—but he had! And I could not forget it. I gave him my heart, and he left it behind.

I felt like the branches of the oak. Constantly trying to reach for a peace I could not attain. The roots in the ground and the constant shift of the wind continually thwarted my progress to find heaven.

CHAPTER 7
Mr. Charles Brumley

❧

DUTIES AT RIVERTON PARK INHIBITED me from calling at Astoria the following day, but Leah still consumed my thoughts. Her manners were always so easy, her eyes a constant struggle between her heart and mind. How did she continually hold this spell over me?

It was perhaps premature, but I determined to ask Mr. Hastings permission to court his daughter. It was the true reason I had come home, after all. Upon my next visit to Astoria, Leah was brushing down her mare outside the stables when I approached.

She looked up from her task and noticed me. "That is a beautiful horse, Mr. Brumley," she said. Or maybe she noticed my horse.

I dismounted and handed the reins to the groom. "Thank you. Mouse is the most recent addition to my stables."

"Mouse?" she repeated with a laugh.

"Of course. What else would you name your horse?"

Leah shook her head and agreed to let me escort her back to the house. As we walked, she breathed deeply and tilted her head back to absorb the sun on her face. I'd always admired how she could appreciate the simple pleasures of life.

She paused, and my eyes were pulled to her. With her eyes closed and her face serene, I wanted to stare, to hold her sun-strewn cheeks in my hands. Instead, I clasped my fingers tightly behind my back and respectfully returned my eyes to the path. "Tell me about your season," I asked. "You came to London when I was at Landers Lodge." Leah knew that every fall my family visited our property in Nottinghamshire. I had often wondered if she had selected her presentation to the ton, knowing I would be absent. It would have been enlightening to see her interact with the gentry and to hear her candid observations.

Leah opened her eyes and turned towards me. She pulled off her gloves and shrugged. "It was as I expected."

"You enjoyed the diversions of London?"

"The diversions filled their purpose, I suppose." She got a mischievous look in her eye. "I found I rather enjoyed watching the game play out."

"Game?"

Leah rolled her eyes. "The marriage mart. All of those elegant ladies and their *mothers*." She raised her eyebrows to emphasize her point. She was right: the ladies themselves could be presumptuous and forward, but the mothers were worse than gaggling hens.

"I suppose for an unconcerned female it might provide entertainment. Yet it's a dreadful reality for those attempting to win its . . . spoils."

"I didn't refer to it as a war, Mr. Brumley, simply a game."

A battle was a far more accurate analogy, but I followed her lead. "A game that ends with the selection of a spouse, a lifelong partner. I would hope when you are ready to enter the play you will not be so foolhardy as to treat it lightly. Given your face, your dowry, and your innocence, you are likely to wind up swindled by some handsome rake."

"A handsome rake?" Leah grinned and raised her eyebrows. "I didn't realize you had entered the game, Mr. Brumley. For, while I have not seen you these many months, a girl does hear things."

My feet froze as dread inched through my chest. "Are you insinuating that I need to defend my reputation as a gentleman?"

Leah's amused eyes held mine for a short moment. She seemed to be searching for something. Then she slid her gaze towards the house. "No, admittedly that is the only reputation I have heard of." The timbre of her voice dropped as she returned her eyes to mine and dramatically imperson-ated her father. "Mr. Brumley is all the rage at Cambridge. The professors are astounded by his intellect. Mrs. Brumley could not be more proud."

My shoulders relaxed. It was good to have her tease me again. I had missed it.

We walked in silence. Then in almost a whisper, she said, "I thought for sure I would hear of some beauty on your arm."

After a few steps more, I turned and offered a quick bow to Leah. Then I raised my arm. She considered my invitation for a moment before slipping her hand through. She barely rested her fingers on my coat sleeve, but it warmed me to my heart. I considered it another small sign that I could hope.

"Now you may deem yourself a witness to the beauty on my arm," I said with a smile.

Leah slipped her arm free, and the gravel crunched beneath her boots as she stepped on the garden path. "You, Mr. Brumley, are still a tease."

"And you, Miss Leah, claimed I was a rake."

Leah lowered her chin, and I noticed her foot begin to tap beneath the hem of her riding habit. "I apologize, Mr. Brumley. For while it's true that you tease, you did not deserve the insult."

My finger moved to her chin, lifting it until her speckled brown eyes met mine. "You are forgiven." I cocked my head, hoping for some confirmation that her feelings for me had not been entirely extinguished. The urge to touch her again, to say something more, brewed in my core. My finger fell from her face, and I leaned forward to speak, but the words caught in my throat. Could she not feel the electricity between us? Surely it was not my heartbeat alone that quickened.

"Thank you, my friend," Leah said.

Friend.

The word doused any warmth I'd felt, replacing it with a brittle chill. The coolness moved towards my heart while we continued our stroll. I allowed the cold to move through me, into my veins, reaching every corner of my body. And when I was completely numb, I asked the question I knew I must. "I'm sure the gentlemen were enthralled with you."

Leah did not answer.

"Anyone in particular? Captain Wilkins, perhaps?" I prodded, willing that coolness to pool inside. A slight blush stole across her cheeks, and a sharp pang of jealousy shot through me.

"There was nothing of significance to report." Leah's eyes remained forward, watching her footfalls on the path.

"Your change in complexion would suggest otherwise."

The gravel ground beneath her heel as she fiercely turned to face me. "Mr. Brumley, I cannot discuss this with you."

"Come now, Miss Leah, you know I will rail you no more than Ferrin." This was torture. My heart beat erratically in my chest, but I had to know. "Do you have an attachment to someone?"

Leah's eyes scolded me. "If I were being courted, you would know."

She advanced the next few steps in silence, quiet and almost sorrowful. Then it was as if a candle had lit inside her. She stood straight and said, "I will tell you that Father approves of Sarah's upcoming engagement."

"A valiant attempt at turning the subject, Miss Leah, but I will not be swayed." I could not stop now; although my inquiry could prove disastrous. I turned and blocked her way. "His name?"

Leah's eyes shot open wide. She tried to step around me. With every step she took, I matched her footfalls and blocked her again. She shifted left then a quick step to the right. I frustrated her every attempt.

"One word is all I require." I hoped to tease the truth from her.

She stomped her foot and threw her hands down in fists to her sides. "Let me pass!"

Laughter erupted from within me. "I'm glad to see you have not changed, my dear."

Pushing my shoulder, she knocked me off balance and growled as she walked past. The effect was opposite of what she desired. I laughed harder then quickened my pace to return to her side.

I calmed myself with a deep breath. "It's good to have you back, Leah."

She spun around on the back stairs, and through her clenched jaw, she spat at me, "You may have *come* back, Mr. Brumley, but you most definitely do not have *me* back."

The shock her words sent through me stilled my steps. I had pushed too far. Why couldn't I be satisfied walking with her on my arm? We had enjoyed a real conversation until I got selfish and wanted more. It could have been a lovely new beginning, but instead I watched her walk inside, each footfall of her pounding boots crushing my heart a little more. What was I to do?

CHAPTER 8
Miss Leah Hastings

MY BURNING FRUSTRATION WOULD NOT cease despite the tepid water I splashed on my face. One moment he could be so charming and the next, insufferable! It had always been like that, and I don't know why I expected any change. Charles would tease smiles from me then laugh when he pushed things too far. I often felt that I was a game to him. There had been a time when I didn't mind playing along. There had been a time when I could hold my head high and tease him right back. We would banter, yet we could always balance our emotions and separate the serious from the nonsensical.

When he made me truly angry, he would think of some way to earn my forgiveness: a handpicked bouquet of forget-me-nots, an extra bone for Admiral. Once, he even composed a silly rhyme. I forgave him every time until the last. I could forgive him for playing games with my smiles, not for playing games with my heart.

I had offered him all of me, and he had made his choice.

My walls needed to be secure. I needed to shore them up so that no matter what he did, I would not forget. I was afraid to forget because if I did, I might have to endure the pain all over again, and once was enough.

Sarah agreed to join me on a walk to Paddington. We reached the end of the lane, and I glanced west towards Riverton Park. I had nearly succeeded in pushing Charles completely from my mind before his return. I rarely recalled our numerous races along these well-worn roads or through the copse of trees situated on the knoll one quarter mile back—the knoll we often claimed as our castle and defended its capture from multitudes of imagined intruders. I rarely reflected on the time I caught three snapping trout and Charles only fished a mangled branch from the pond. And I never, *ever* thought about how once upon a time I had fancied myself in love with Charles Christopher Brumley.

Turning back to the road, I felt proud that I could push those memories away again. Or perhaps I was too proud to admit that I didn't actually want to forget them at all.

No matter.

Determination to focus on something other than Charles moved me forward. I slipped my arm through Sarah's. "Tell me about Mr. Dashel."

Sarah seemed startled by my request. She even colored a little, which I considered a sign that she was truly in love. It took a lot to disconcert my sister.

"What do you wish to know?" she asked, walking regally beside me.

"Everything!" I raised my chin and waved my free arm at the open road before us.

"Leah," Sarah chastised. "I do not wish to be mocked."

I pretended to be offended. "I am not mocking you. Honestly!" I laughed; then in a more sober tone, I said, "If I am soon to call him brother, I ought to know a little about him."

Sarah looked down at me, judging the sincerity of my request. She must have found my pleading eyes convincing enough. Her face softened as she began to describe her beau. "Mr. Dashel is very handsome, but that was not what first caught my attention." She watched my expression, and I gave her a small smile to let her know I believed her. Sarah was beautiful, but she had never been vain.

"I was attending a concert with Aunt and Uncle Barnes at the home of their friend Mrs. Cottsworth. Mr. Dashel has a sister who's twenty, your age, and he was escorting her that evening. They sat behind us, and while I knew who they were, I had not yet made their acquaintance. As you know, the marriage mart can be quite"—she bobbed her head searching for the right word—"intimidating." She suppressed her laugh with the back of her hand. Sarah removed her fingers from her lips and continued. "As the guests were getting settled, I overheard a conversation."

"Eavesdropping, Sarah? I did not fathom you the type." I clicked my tongue and feigned disapproval.

"It was a crowded room and cannot be considered eavesdropping since I was in plain sight." She nudged my side with her elbow but continued to hold my arm in hers.

This was how our relationship worked. When we got on, we got on well. It was just far too often that we were out of sorts with one another. But I never doubted we loved each other.

Sarah continued. "I heard a man request the seat next to Miss Dashel. Mr. Dashel dismissed the gentleman, yet he did it in such a way that there could be no offense taken. I turned to see the man walk away and was shocked to see it was Lord Everett."

"And pray tell, who is Lord Everett?" The name meant nothing to me.

"Lord Everett is a walking contradiction. He is one of the most sought-after bachelors in Town and one of the most notorious rakes."

"So in snubbing Lord Everett, Mr. Dashel was protecting his sister."

"Yes, which I would expect any respectable older brother to do. But, Leah," she actually sighed, "it was the way he deferred Lord Everett. It wasn't a snub or an insult. He addressed him kindly and directly; I knew in that moment I wanted to know more about this humble, unpretentious man."

"So you are very much alike," I said pointedly.

Sarah's face colored slightly again. "I wish I could claim his good graces. We have many similar tastes, but I lack his unyielding patience." We walked a few more steps in silence. "There are numerous times I wished I would have been more patient with you, dear sister." She squeezed my hand.

"Ah, and there is that humility you spoke about." I snuggled her arm closer to mine.

Sarah sighed again. "Mr. Dashel has the most exquisite brown eyes."

I laughed. "Please don't swoon in the road. I don't have the strength to drag you back home again."

As Sarah pondered on her beloved, I could see the joy in her countenance. The wide smile spread across her face reflected the happiness filling her soul. My own heart swelled to see her so completely in raptures, and I felt a twinge of jealousy. My eyes returned to the road as a pair of rogue leaves blew in front of us.

Not long ago I had hoped for the same sort of happiness. I enjoyed my time with Captain Wilkins—I truly did—but our relationship was missing that magical current, the something more that would define our feelings as love.

I knew what it felt like because, not long ago, my heart had beat and pulsed with the very acute feeling—a combination of raptures and excitement and joy all bubbling together inside and pushing to break free from the confines of my body. The intoxicating combination spread throughout all of me, from the palms of my hands down to the soles of my feet, yearning to see that special someone again, longing for every moment we could steal away. I savored every memory and every touch.

I had been completely smitten. Yes, there was a time when I had known what it meant to love and to love wholly. Sarah now reflected that same emotion, yet it was one I found myself entirely depleted of.

Captain Wilkins was a good man. He treated me kindly. I felt safe in his presence, and I was certain we felt an attraction to one another. Yet he did not elicit in me the rapturous bliss I now saw in Sarah.

"How did you know you loved him?" I asked. My serious tone broke the moment, and I immediately tried to lighten the mood. "Besides his 'exquisite brown eyes,' I mean?"

Sarah shrugged. "I'm not sure I can describe it. When I'm with Mr. Dashel, I feel an unexplainable joy." She placed her hand on her heart. "And when we are apart, I ache with longing to see him and feel that comfort again." Sarah dropped her arms and wrapped them around herself. "He makes me feel whole."

Did I feel complete with Captain Wilkins? Appreciated, yes. Admired, yes. But whole?

Our first stop in Paddington was to frank Sarah's letter to our aunt in London. They had agreed upon a date for Sarah's return. She would travel to London in just under a fortnight. There she could reunite with Mr. Dashel and feel whole again. I smiled at the thought.

We stopped at the inn to take nuncheon and then perused the ribbon shop. Sarah found a bonnet she liked at the milliner's and determined to ask Father to buy it for her trip to London.

The wind grew violent as we walked home. Its impatient thrashing pulled at our gowns and coats, sweeping us sideways on the road.

"We should have ordered the carriage for our excursion today," Sarah shouted above the wind, holding a hand on her head to keep her bonnet in place.

A tempestuous gale thrust me off balance, and my legs became tangled in my skirts. I reached out to steady myself and instead managed to tackle Sarah to the ground and crumple on top of her.

"Leah!" She pushed me off to the side.

Bunches of fabric entwined my legs, and I laughed helplessly as I rolled free of her flailing limbs. My bonnet had fallen off, and I tried to pull my feet beneath me. While attempting to stand, I fell backwards again and laughed harder. Sarah had righted herself and leaned over to lend me a hand when the sound of an approaching carriage caused us to look down the lane in unison.

It was not our carriage, but one we knew well—Mr. Brumley's.

The equipage pulled alongside us. My giggles continued as Mr. Brumley alighted. I tried to bite on my lips to tame my laughter.

"Miss Hastings," he addressed Sarah. "Why is your sister prostrate on the side of the road?"

One look at his confused expression, and my resolve was lost. Laughter erupted, and I could not contain it. Sarah placed her hands on her hips and tried to shame me with a matronly glare. I only laughed harder. Mr. Brumley's mouth turned up into a smile. My eyes watered from the entire debacle.

Charles walked over, squatted in front of me, and handed me his handkerchief. Then placing one hand on my elbow and the other on my side, he assisted me to my feet.

I took several awkward steps and almost fell again.

"Whoa," Charles said, pulling me close to him.

His breath brushed my cheek, and I realized how near he stood and how tightly he held me. The air froze in my lungs. I halted my giggles and stood completely still. My feet were no longer swaying beneath me; I was now stable and grounded. At the same time, I felt weightless. I was not aware of my legs, only of Charles's arm anchored firmly around my waist. He stood directly behind me, and his warmth pressed against my back.

While I was certain I wouldn't fall again, my heart spun dizzily in my chest and my thoughts tangled in my head. A sacred spell had descended on us. It resembled the magic I had reflected on earlier. The comedy from moments before suddenly evolved into an upsetting epiphany. My palms tingled, my toes tingled, and I felt breathless and delirious with a joy that was no longer from tumbling on the ground. I loved Charles Brumley! I had loved him before, and I could not deny that I loved him still. I loved standing with his arm around me, leaning into him and feeling his nearness.

I finally took a breath so I would not pass out. The wind seemed to die away, and when I turned to look at Charles, I found him perfectly still, staring back at me. A smile touched the corners of his mouth, and I desperately wanted him to close the distance between us and kiss me.

Sarah broke the tranquility. "Are you quite yourself again?" she asked with prevalent chastisement.

My eyes closed in an effort to regain my composure. I pulled out of Charles's arm, and the hand he held on my elbow slid down to grasp my fingers.

"Thank you, Mr. Brumley." I squeezed his hand but did not let go. I could not bring myself to completely sever the connection.

He regarded me thoughtfully but said nothing. The questions in his eyes were too numerous to delineate. And then he released his grip, and the magic was gone. "May I escort you ladies home?" Charles turned towards Sarah for an answer.

"It would be greatly appreciated."

Charles handed us into the carriage and sat on the bench opposite Sarah and me. My sister did a commendable job of discussing socially neutral topics and inquiring after the affairs at Riverton Park. I contributed a small smile or head nod when my input was requested, but otherwise I focused out the window, watching the wind tear the leaves from their branches.

The trees fought to cling to their hard-earned foliage. The determined wind so easily tore away the efforts of the entire year. The leaves never stood a chance, and I wondered if my heart ever had a chance to forget my brown-eyed friend and the tingles he could elicit from my heart.

I wandered through the gardens, contemplating the meaning of my revelation the day before. I loved Charles. I was sure of it. I was sure I would always love him, but I had long ago dismissed any notion that I would gain his affection in return. When he disappeared a year ago, it broke my heart. I had no intention of allowing my emotions to win this battle. I could suppress my heart and move on.

Captain Wilkins was an admirable, attractive man who was interested in me. I simply would not let Charles ruffle me. I could be stubborn and determined. Now my heart just needed to cooperate.

A movement on the path caught my eye. "Admiral!" I welcomed the caramel-colored dog with both hands and was rewarded with an excited head nudge that almost knocked me off my feet.

Mr. Brumley suddenly appeared next to me, bracing me with a firm hand until my feet caught under me once again.

"Mr. Brumley? It seems you have rescued me again." Stepping away from him, I determined to not get fluttery. "What brings you to Astoria today?"

He ignored my question. "Admiral?" he asked.

"The very same one you tortured," I said and knelt down to stroke Admiral's soft fur.

"There was no torture involved. Just a slight swimming test," Charles refuted as he gave Admiral a hearty rub.

"Which he has since passed," said a voice from behind us. We both stood and turned to greet Father.

"Mr. Hastings." Charles offered the appropriate bow.

"Brumley." Father narrowed his eyes at Charles, and I hoped it made him squirm. "I understand you've been a frequent visitor these past weeks."

"As you know, sir, I have been long away from Derbyshire and find that I have truly missed many of the country's treasures." When Father raised his eyebrows, Mr. Brumley cleared his throat and continued. "However, rather than impede on your generous hospitality again, I was hoping to return the favor. My mother is hosting a dinner tomorrow at Riverton Park, and she insists that I invite your lovely family to join us."

Father looked at me. My jaw clenched tight, and I tried to keep my expression neutral. It was only dinner. He turned back to Mr. Brumley. "Tell your mother we would be happy to accept."

Mr. Brumley bowed again then turned towards me. "Until tomorrow, then."

I flexed my toes in my boots and offered the tiniest of curtsies. I would not tingle or flutter for Mr. Brumley. I must keep my heart under strict censure.

I wore my favorite dinner gown simply because it was my favorite. Soft yellow, trimmed with ribbon a shade darker so the gown appeared to be kissed by the sun. Gerty wove a matching ribbon through my braids; a few dark curls escaped the pins and hung loose on my neck.

As we entered the drawing room at Riverton Park, I realized the gathering was much larger than I had assumed. Mr. and Mrs. Harrison from the local parish were conversing with Mrs. Brumley. Mr. Brumley was talking to Rachel and Mr. Ansley.

Miss Ansley sat across the room sharing a settee with her mother, who was watching Charles's every move. When Ferrin entered, his face revealed his immediate admiration of Miss Ansley and her beauty. The absurdity of this game made me want to laugh. Mrs. Ansley turned her eyes from Mr. Brumley and offered me an immediate scowl.

Mr. Brumley noted our arrival and walked over. He addressed Father first, then Ferrin, Aunt Evelyn, Sarah, and myself. My family proceeded through the entryway, and upon my passing Charles, he whispered how lovely I looked. My cheeks darkened, and I stepped away from him, pretending to admire a painting in a secluded corner. I would not let him ruffle me.

Dinner was announced, and Mr. Brumley escorted his mother into the dining room. The remaining guests followed, with Ferrin giddily escorting Miss Ansley.

Sarah entered gracefully on her own, properly following protocol, of course. But I could not resist grabbing Rachel's arm through mine. I raised my chin in faux superiority as we followed the rest of the party through the door. Rachel giggled, causing the ire of Mrs. Ansley and an exorbitant eye roll from dear Aunt Evelyn. Somehow I kept my face passive as I deposited Rachel in her seat with a proper bow.

There was no reason for me to feel inferior. These were my friends, the individuals that filled my childhood memories. I would enjoy this night and not let bitter Mrs. Ansley or conceited Mr. Brumley corrode another memory.

My epiphany sat tenderly on my mind, but I had secured the walls around my heart, and I was determined to move on. Charles was my friend; he would always be my friend, for his heart was destined elsewhere and so was mine.

CHAPTER 9
Mr. Charles Brumley

WHEN LEAH LED RACHEL INTO the dining room like a haughty peacock, I stood behind my chair trying to remain impassive, but the far right corner of my mouth betrayed me. The aching in my chest returned. That feeling from long ago confirmed I was in trouble. Leah had my heart in her clutches, and I was helpless. She alone would decide whether she would crush it or embrace it.

I tried to give Mrs. Ansley the proper courtesies of conversation throughout the meal; however, my gaze—and attention—continued to wander to the end of the table where Leah sat. I pictured Leah with Rachel on her arm and inevitably my grin returned.

"Come, Mr. Brumley," Mrs. Ansley said. "What has made you smile?"

"'Tis nothing, Mrs. Ansley." I turned towards her and tried to focus my attention on my food.

"Perhaps Catherine's new gown?" The woman's smile pinched her round cheeks and tiny mouth together in a small oval. "Don't you think it's lovely? And complements her so well?" Mrs. Ansley's shrill voice had ceased all other conversation. It amazed me that something so loud could originate from such a small figure.

All eyes were suddenly fixed upon me, awaiting my response. "It is indeed a lovely gown, Mrs. Ansley." I forced a smile and turned to my food, anxious to move the conversation elsewhere.

However, Mrs. Ansley continued. "And the shade? Complements her skin perfectly, don't you agree? Subtle and proper, unlike those obnoxious, bright tones that some ladies consider to be the rage." She quickly glanced towards the end of the table, shifted in her seat, and squared her shoulders.

"Yes, blue does complement gentle features. Many a pretty face have chosen that color, as it is hard to go wrong with blue." Mrs. Ansley opened her mouth to say something more, but I quickly continued. "Yet I find it refreshing and a bit daring to try a bold, bright hue, something warm and radiant like the sun." Mother's rebuke filled her eyes, but it was too late. With feigned innocence I turned my eyes back to Mrs. Ansley and her gaping jaw.

Mrs. Clem suddenly choked on her venison. Thankfully, she calmed her convulsions and Mother provided a diversion. "You must try this trifle," she said. "Our cook, Mrs. Rowe, makes the most exquisite trifle." And with that, dessert was served.

With the trifle consumed, the women retired to the drawing room. I saw no need and had no desire to linger after the meal and thus led the gentlemen to join the rest of the party. Mr. Ansley joined Mrs. Brumley, Mr. Hastings, and Mrs. Clem for a game of whist. Mr. and Mrs. Harrison engaged Rachel in conversation; Ferrin, Sarah, and Miss Ansley were sharing some joke in the corner. I approached Leah, who stood alone against the far wall.

"That was quite an entrance to dinner, Miss Leah," I said as I walked up.

"You will never know what it is like to be relegated to the back of the procession, Mr. Brumley. I was simply trying to impress upon dear Rachel that it does not need to be as dull as it may seem."

In that same instant, Rachel squealed her delight at something Mrs. Harrison said. I chuckled at her innocent exuberance then turned to admire Leah's profile. "I'd say you accomplished your goal."

The candles on the sconce behind Leah illuminated her rogue tendrils of hair, framing the rich brown with a golden halo. My eyes found hers again, and happiness surged through me. My gaze wandered from her eyes down her face to her lips, which twisted up in a feisty smile. My heart raced. How I'd dreamed of that smile, those lips turned up in joy, just for me.

After clearing my throat, I spoke again. "Did I tell you that you look lovely tonight?"

Leah looked pointedly at me. Her smile faded and was replaced by indifference. I could not account for the sudden change. "Yes, you did, Mr. Brumley. And again, I thank you. Please excuse me."

She made to leave, but feeling bold, I grabbed her arm, leaned closer, and whispered in her ear, "I relish the bit of sunshine you have provided this evening."

In that moment, it felt as if the sun really was streaming through the curtains. Warmth and invigoration seeped through my limbs. Leah closed her eyes briefly, and when she opened them again they lowered to the ground. She shook her arm free of my hold and shivered. Could she not feel the heat between us?

"Are you cold?" I asked.

"No," Leah said softly. "You must excuse me."

"Ahem." Mrs. Ansley approached from behind. She turned her icy eyes on Leah, and the warmth of the moment vanished. "Will you be favoring us at the pianoforte tonight?"

I snickered aloud and quickly raised a hand to cover my grin. Music had never been Leah's strength.

"No," Leah replied with fire in her eyes. "As you are aware, Mrs. Ansley, I am not fortunate enough to count the pianoforte among the talents I possess."

"Hmm, what a shame," Mrs. Ansley said, though her mischievous eyes defied any true remorse. "Then perhaps my Catherine can provide a piece or two?" Her eyes shifted to me, waiting for a reply.

"That would be delightful," I said. Mother would certainly give me a tongue lashing if I crossed Mrs. Ansley once more.

The conniving woman spoke again. "It would be unseemly for *me* to encourage her to play; it might appear as if I were pressing her to show off, and she would dismiss my request at once." She flicked her wrist, and before I knew it, her fan was pressed against my waistcoat. "However, if you, Mr. Brumley, could invite her to share her bountiful talents, I'm sure she would agree." Her wrist flipped again, and in the next second Mrs. Ansley wore a kind smile while she slowly stirred the air with her fan spread wide.

Left with no alternative, I excused myself to relay my coerced desires.

CHAPTER 10
Miss Leah Hastings

❧❦☙

THE FLAMES SIMMERING BENEATH MY skin surrendered to the chill that Mrs. Ansley no doubt intended to impart. When Charles grabbed my arm, it was all I could do to pull away. My shivers stemmed from delight. I did not want to feel fire from his touch. I did not want to feel the intensity his presence brought. I meant to walk away. I had almost accomplished my purpose when Mrs. Ansley approached.

Perhaps I should thank her for physically separating us, but as she had been so underhanded in accomplishing her goal, it irked me.

Mrs. Ansley stood by my side and watched Charles approach her daughter. "They make a handsome couple, don't you agree, Miss Leah?" she hissed in my ear.

Mr. Brumley laughed with Miss Ansley. I replied, "As both are handsome individuals, reason would suggest that they would indeed make a handsome couple."

"Do not play daft, Miss Leah." Mrs. Ansley raised her fan to conceal her ice-cold words. "It's well known that you have been monopolizing Mr. Brumley since his return to Riverton Park. Since such a match would certainly not benefit him, I can only assume you are leading him on quite improperly with your wily ways."

I actually gasped at her accusation and found myself frozen and unable to articulate a single word in reply.

"Do not suppose that he will be making an offer to you. Catherine is the one he shall marry," Mrs. Ansley sneered.

Charles and Catherine moved to the piano. After Catherine was seated, Charles stood beside her to make sure she was settled; as he stepped away, he raised an eyebrow at me as if we shared a secret joke. His gesture melted the frost that had fallen over me, and I turned towards Mrs. Ansley.

"I must disagree with your assumption that I have nothing to offer Mr. Brumley, as you are well aware of my family and my dowry. It is certainly no secret that he and I are friends and longtime acquaintances. If he has been monopolized, as you claim, I wonder why *he* does not set it right? Poor Catherine, to be scandalized by Mr. Brumley." I paused purposefully and took a timed breath before continuing. "That is, if they are properly courting, as you claim."

"Miss Leah, you are every bit as stubborn now as when you were a child, a trait, no doubt, inherited from your father. It seems I have no choice but to remind you that your family name is on a shaky foundation at best. Your father's stubbornness cost the life of your dear mother."

Her words effectively shocked me.

"Excuse me?" My eyes met hers, and I loathed her confident smirk.

"Oh yes, I know the truth. I know there was time to fetch the doctor. I know her maid begged him to go, and he refused. Time was precious, and he selfishly stayed by her side as she died." Mrs. Ansley's cold eyes held me spellbound.

"Where did you hear that?" My throat tightened.

"Ah, how it came to me does not signify. It is true enough, as you well know." A smirk spread across her pointy features.

I glanced at my father. He smiled at the players seated at the table, sharing in some joke. With steeled eyes I looked hard at Mrs. Ansley.

She ignored my glaring reproach. "Only a few people know the particulars of what happened that night. I see you are one of them, as am I. It would be a shame if the truth were more widely circulated. Your father's reputation would suffer immeasurably. There would no doubt be some sort of spiritual repercussion, as Mr. Harrison could not be in association with such a gentleman." She closed her fan and tapped it against her open palm while she turned her icy gaze to my father. "I wonder if there would be legal ramifications as well. I'm not sure your family could survive such scandal. It would be a shame to see Sarah's upcoming betrothal come to naught." Her steely gaze turned to me once again.

"You have made your point, Mrs. Ansley," I snapped with renewed hatred.

She raised her fan again. "Stay away from Mr. Brumley, and I'm sure this will go no further."

"As I told you, we are simply friends."

"Then my conditions shall hold no hindrance. But if not—your father's role may become more widely circulated." Mrs. Ansley snapped her fan shut and walked to the pianoforte. She pressed her pointed lips into a smile and loudly doted compliments on her daughter's abilities.

Mr. Brumley whipped his head around, and looking past Mrs. Ansley, he eyed me suspiciously.

With a weak smile, I approached my aunt Evelyn. A sudden headache had accosted me, and I needed her to escort me home.

CHAPTER 11
Mr. Charles Brumley

❧

DURING MISS ANSLEY'S PIANO PIECE, Leah disappeared. Her aunt relayed the excuse of a headache to my mother, and both ladies departed.

I found it curious that Leah's headache presented itself after her conversation with Mrs. Ansley, and I wondered if the devious woman had played a role in Leah's sudden departure.

The evening was fraught with Mrs. Ansley's praises piled high and loud upon her daughter. Miss Ansley looked unnerved every time her mother spoke. The constant cacophony did sound rather like a braying mule. Miss Ansley was pretty, but her mother's incessant bragging had a damaging effect, stripping her daughter of the confidence that would allow her true beauty to shine.

There was success in the evening only because I had at last secured a time to ask Mr. Hastings for permission to court his daughter. Both Hastings men and Mr. Ansley would arrive midmorning to hunt pheasants on my estate. I was determined to get Mr. Hastings alone and finally be granted permission to court the woman who had won my heart so long ago. Hopefully Leah would forgive me for my folly of the year past.

CHAPTER 12
Miss Leah Hastings

෴

THE FOLLOWING MORNING WHEN I entered the breakfast room, Father sat reading the paper.

"Are you feeling well this morning, dear Leah?" he asked. "Headache gone?"

"Much improved, thank you." I placed some eggs and a muffin on my plate and sat near my father at the table.

He set his paper aside. "Glad to hear it. Brumley has been so kind as to invite Ferrin and me to hunt with him today. We are to leave in a quarter hour."

I gave Father a slight smile and turned my attention to my food in an attempt to push away any thought related to Mr. Brumley. A dull throbbing still drummed through my temples, and my appetite disappeared. I spread the eggs around on my plate, willing them to disappear.

Father pushed himself up from the table. "I have a good feeling about today. I think it will be . . ." he paused and tapped his finger on his lower lip, "quite productive." His plump cheeks rose in a smile full of expectation.

Father's ambiguity confused me. He laughed as he strode into the hall and called for his horse.

Since Mother's passing, Father's moments of levity were few and far between. As of late, he had been extremely chipper, which was one more reason for me not to reveal Mrs. Ansley's coldhearted blackmail. I preferred my father's joviality much more than the somber blue devils that encroached when he thought about Mother. There was no reason to dwell on her passing or to even mention Mrs. Ansley's threat. He must enjoy his day of hunting and all the expectation he held with it.

I was reading late in the library when I heard Father and Ferrin return home. With a candle in hand, I peeked into the hallway. Just before Father crossed the threshold of his study, my light caught his attention.

"Good evening, my dear. Please, come join me." He stepped through the doorway before I could reply.

Father lounged against the mantel and poked at the remains of a fire. He stirred the embers then returned the poker to its place and stepped around his oil-stained walnut desk.

"How was the hunt?" I asked.

Father sat in his imposing leather chair and motioned me to the one opposite him. Once I was seated, he said, "The hunt went well. Nothing of grandeur to report. Ferrin and I bagged a few birds." Then he chuckled to himself.

"Is that a laugh you wish to share?" I asked.

"No, no." Father waved my inquiry aside. "I was thinking of Mr. Ansley." He laughed again.

"And what do you find so amusing about him?"

Father attempted to be serious with a heavy sigh. "He has a decent shot, Mr. Ansley—" He laughed again and shook his head. "I'm sorry. Truly he does, but he has an aversion to noise. He could not hold his weapon while the rest of us continued to shoot." Father rubbed his hand over his eyes. "He started every time a shot rang out and sorely missed every target. He made for a sorry sight, indeed." Father shook his head at the memory.

I could imagine the scene. Mr. Ansley was a good man who was *almost* good at many things, but he excelled at none.

Father wiped at his eyes and straightened himself in his chair. "Mr. Ansley gave me a good laugh today, he did." He chuckled one more time then waved away his amusement. "Anyway, that is not why I called you in here. You see, as promised, the day was productive."

Curiosity nudged me forward in my chair.

"Upon our return to the house, Mr. Brumley asked for a word—in private." Father raised his hand to his lowered chin and crossed his long legs. When I did not respond, he went on. "He first invited us to join him for a hunt at his home in Notinghamshire, Landers Lodge." My father paused, and when I remained silent, he continued. "I assume you are aware of the other matter he wanted to discuss?"

"On the contrary, Father. I've no idea." My stomach tightened, and my foot began to swing involuntarily under my skirt as my hands tangled in my lap.

My father did not speak but eyed me suspiciously. I finally clutched my hands together, willed them to hold still, and forced my gaze to hold his.

"Does that mean you are unaware of Mr. Brumley's interest in you?" Father asked.

"Interest?" Oh, my! As soon as the word left my lips, realization hit me. I did know. I wasn't sure when or how, but now, without a doubt, I knew. My breath was short. "I . . . I . . ." I didn't know what to say.

How did I not see it before? His questions at the ball, his multiple visits, his dismissal of Captain Wilkins—was that the proof? When he held me close on the side of the road, he did hold me longer than necessary. My heartbeat sped at the memory. His hand had pulled me closer, and at dinner he specifically sought me out and paid me compliments. There had been something there before Mrs. Ansley's interruption. My heart fell—Mrs. Ansley! My eyes clamped shut as the coldness of her threat effectively doused any spark of hope.

"Leah, Mr. Brumley asked permission to court you," Father said.

Shock jolted me out of my seat. I walked to the window.

"I thought you would be pleased," he said softly.

With my back to my father, I wrung my hands once again. "But we are only friends." My heart crumpled at the words.

The room was silent except for the embers simmering in the hearth. My fingers began to ache from squeezing them so hard. "What did you tell him?" I asked on a whispered breath. My eyes returned to my father.

He placed his fingers under his chin again and stared at me for a long minute before he lowered his hands to his lap. "I told him yes."

My eyelids fluttered rapidly, and a small cry escaped my throat.

"I'm sorry, my dear. With the recent attentions paid by Brumley, combined with your friendship in the past, I had always assumed . . ." His voice trailed off, and then Father crinkled his brow. "Brumley would make a good husband, would he not?"

"Yes!" I declared around the tightness in my throat. "Mr. Brumley will make a wonderful husband," my voice shuttered, "for someone." And he would. Despite all of the teasing, he was a good man. A good man who excelled in a great *many* things.

Father looked at me with concern. "But not for you?"

I shook my head while I fervently blinked to hold back the tears. Mr. Brumley, Charles, had asked to court me. Me! Was that what I wanted? My heart sped like the wings of a hummingbird. Whether for fear of Mrs. Ansley or because my heart was ready to take flight, I did not know. Charles, my friend, my best friend.

This was what I had dreamed of only one year ago, but now it was all wrong. Another whimper escaped, and my hands moved to cover my trembling lips.

"Leah," Father said softly, "you know I want you to be happy. I loved your mother and wish for the same happiness for you. I will not force you into marriage, and if you wish for me to withdraw my permission for Brumley to court you, I will."

Father regarded me kindly, but I avoided his eyes. What was I to say? Charles had a place in my heart. Yet it did not matter if I wanted to be with him because Mrs. Ansley had extinguished any possibility of a future between us. My gaze turned back to the window, and my eyes pressed closed.

Father misunderstood my hesitation. "I thought you were over that Captain Watkins."

"Captain *Wilkins*." The correction came unconsiously. "And—oh!" I began to pace in front of the window. To accept Mr. Brumley's request would mean my father's ruin. Mrs. Ansley had made her terms clear.

Memories of that night flooded me anew. Mother thrashed with her raging fever. Dr. Hutchins had called earlier in the day. He would not guarantee Mother a full recovery, but he had given us hope in her continued improvement. He offered to stay the night, but Father sent him away. Father was certain she would recuperate and be restored to health in a day or two. I accepted Father's assurance blissfully, believing in his strong confidence.

Then she took a turn for the worse. Both Sarah and I ran in when we heard the commotion. Mother's maid, Louisa, had tried to shoo us from the room. She ushered Sarah away and enlisted her to intercept Ferrin. I ducked behind Louisa's back and hid in the dressing room. I cracked open the door and saw Mother writhing in pain. Father knelt beside her bed, holding her hand in his, stroking it and speaking calmly, as though if he had enough patience or remained there long enough, he could talk the fever out of her. He turned, and I saw the tears running down his face. I knew. I knew he had surrendered and that my mother would never again rise from her bed.

"Call Dr. Hutchins!" Louisa begged my father. "Please, sir. Send for the doctor."

Father did not answer. He just shook his head, stroking her hand; calmly he proclaimed his love for her through his tears.

It was a memory I had buried deep, because when it rose to the surface, it burned fresh and raw. Now, looking out the windows of Father's study, I realized my shoulders were shaking. My arms wrapped around my chest in an attempt to reassure myself that night was over. Mother was gone.

Mrs. Ansley was right. Father did not call Dr. Hutchins. Mother's final moments had been torment mixed with relief. Father sat by her side until the end. And now Mrs. Ansley wished to punish him for it. Mrs. Ansley, who knew nothing of love, nothing of family. My thoughts were uncharitable, but how dare Mrs. Ansley turn that sacred moment into a threat of ruin. Cruel, unfeeling woman!

Oh, what was I to do? My father watched me. Concern creased the corners of his eyes, his mouth drawn down, waiting for my answer. There was simply one response to give.

"You are mistaken, Father." My voice shook. "Captain Wilkins has claim on my heart. I cannot share it with another."

And with those lying words, my heart broke again.

CHAPTER 13
Mr. Charles Brumley

ശ്ര൪ര

AFTER MR. HASTINGS GRANTED HIS permission, I wanted to sprint to the stables, call for my horse, and ride directly to Astoria.

However, I could not behave nonsensically in front of my prospective father-in-law; thus, common sense prevailed and I pushed my enthusiasm all the way down to my boots. Beneath the table I had quietly tapped my toes while I hosted dinner for the small hunting party.

I floated up to bed, slept soundly, and arose early, counting down the minutes until it would be suitable to call on Leah.

Upon the decided hour, I ordered the phaeton harnessed. The route I had taken hundreds of times before felt new and fresh. The crisp air signaled a new beginning, a fresh start to reach the finale I yearned for.

Arriving at Astoria, I handed the reins to the groom and asked him to hold the horse while I introduced myself at the house and prevailed upon Leah to join me for a ride.

Jensen told me she was unavailable.

"Oh," I said, taken aback. My excitement was temporarily quashed, but it quickly sparked again. "Then perhaps I shall return at a later hour?"

"I am afraid Miss Leah is indisposed for the day, Mr. Brumley." Jensen gave a small bow, my signal to excuse myself. My mind was in a state of stupor. I could not seem to turn around and leave.

"I am sorry, sir," Jensen said, bringing my attention around once more. My eyes met his. "Very well, then. Please give her my regards." I descended the steps and turned back once again. "And thank you, Jensen."

His face remained unreadable as he bowed one more time.

I retook the reins of the phaeton and drove home far too recklessly.

CHAPTER 14

Miss Leah Hastings

❧

STANDING IN MY LATE MOTHER's bedroom, I watched Mr. Brumley depart for the third day in a row. He smartly swung himself into the saddle; he was beautiful in that moment—beautiful and sad. He had just met with Father, and Father retracted his permission to court me.

Mr. Brumley turned his mount towards the road.

Our reunion was much too short, and now he would disappear again, perhaps forever. My heart hurt, drumming slowly and painfully in my chest. Good-byes with Charles had always felt like this. It had taken a full year to mend my injured heart and bruised pride when he left before. Until a month ago, I considered my recovery successful. But his reappearance had caused a relapse which set me back nearly to the point of desolation. It mirrored the agony I had felt that dreadful day Charles had walked away from me. That abandonment was nothing compared to my now-shattered heart.

Charles wanted to be with me. He asked to court me. He wanted the exact thing I had dreamt of so many times. Only now, that dream was impossible, and the thought left me in the depths of despair. My fingers pressed against the clear windowpane, the cool clearness sending icy tendrils to my heart, hoping that in some detached way he could feel me say farewell. I hurt so severely.

Instead of riding down the lane, Charles turned his horse towards the house. His face was hidden under his tall hat until he suddenly raised his eyes to my window. I gasped and dropped my hand back to my side. He stared at me while his horse skittered beneath him. His lips pressed firmly together, and I could see the confusion on his face. The pain. He looked at me, stricken, his eyes sad and pleading. Asking why.

It reminded me of the shattering I felt after his rejection. I wanted to explain that I did not refuse him for the sake of revenge. Pain that deep was too much to inflict upon someone purposefully.

If only I could explain. He would laugh at Mrs. Ansley's threat, tell me not to worry, plot some great strategy against my pleadings to the contrary. But I took Mrs. Ansley at her word, and she had threatened my family. I would not sacrifice them. I would not ruin Sarah's happiness or Father's good name or Ferrin's future. If Father was exposed, we would all fall. There was no way to win, and I felt beaten and bruised.

A single tear rolled down my cheek as Charles pressed his knees into the horse's flanks and galloped away.

Mrs. Ansley had won.

The following week at breakfast my appetite was nonexistent. I frequently skipped my morning meal or ate only a few scant bites.

"Now, Leah, it's not as bad as that," Father said one morning.

Sarah rolled her eyes as Father explained that although he had recanted his permission for Mr. Brumley to court me, Charles had reiterated the invitation to Landers Lodge. Considering my acknowledgment that Charles was a friend, Father had no reservation in accepting the offer. I believed he only had hunting on his mind.

"Why are you still planning this excursion?" I asked and begged him to reconsider.

Ferrin finished piling his plate high and turned from the sideboard. "Just because you've slighted the man, Leah, does not mean Father and I cannot enjoy a good hunt."

"The invitation was for the family." I shot a look at Ferrin.

"And so it remains," Father declared. "Brumley assured me that all are still welcome, and he felt no qualms with including both of my daughters in the invitation. Though as you know, Sarah will be leaving to join your aunt and uncle in London." He took a large bite of muffin. A crumb missed his mouth and tumbled onto his plate. With his mouth half full, he said, "I'm sure the Barneses would welcome you as well. And Sarah might enjoy the company."

"You know I have no desire to return to London," I said, rearranging my napkin in my lap. "Perhaps Aunt Evelyn and I could remain here at Astoria?"

"Aunt Evelyn is quite anxious to make the trip. She's been consulting with Mrs. Brumley on which items to pack for the cooler climate." Father took another bite. "Rachel will be there, as well as the Ansleys." My appetite disappeared. "You should have enough female companions to create a happy diversion while we enjoy our sport. Besides, I've heard Landers Lodge is a most exquisite retreat. I admit that after all these years I am quite anxious to see it for myself."

London was not an option. I did not wish to impose upon Aunt and Uncle Barnes, and I had no desire to watch Sarah and her beau make eyes at each other. Plus, I despised the late nights, constant routs, and rancid air in Town. Neither did I want to spend a month in the presence of cantankerous Mrs. Ansley. I could get on well enough with Catherine. And Rachel was always entertaining, but an entire month?

I sighed. These were my neighbors. They were a part of my life, ornery or not, and it was a life with which I was generally pleased. It would be a much more enjoyable holiday without the Ansleys, but if this was to be my lot, I decided it was best to face it head on.

"So what will it be, Leah? Will you join us men for a bit of sport?" Ferrin asked.

"It seems it has already been decided," I said and let my fork clatter onto my plate.

CHAPTER 15
Mr. Charles Brumley

❧❧❦❧❧

I HAD BEEN SURPRISED TO receive the missive that Leah would be joining us at Landers Lodge. I thought she might accompany her sister to London, as she found me such an undesirable companion. Perhaps she decided to come flaunt her indifference. She always claimed she would take revenge for all of my past riling; I just never thought her revenge would make my heart ache so thoroughly. Even Mrs. Rowe's trifle tasted bland, a confirmation I was out of sorts.

Mr. Hastings retraction of his permission rankled thoroughly, but even more disturbing was the fact that Leah didn't bother to tell me herself. Nor did she offer an explanation in any form. Given our history, our memories, the least she owed me was a reason.

Since my return, there were undeniable moments of magic between us. I thought I knew Leah well enough to recognize when she felt the same pull, the same attraction that I did. It was the same allure that had grown through the years, since our childhood, thickening every year with every interaction until the magical concoction was too strong to ignore. But that was exactly what Leah had done. She ignored me. She avoided me for three consecutive days culminating with her father's curt dismissal.

Leah ignored my feelings, and now, without an explanation, an understanding of where we stood, she planned to arrive on my doorstep and play coy games. As a child I enjoyed playing games with Leah. Often enough we were evenly matched and she was generally a good sport. One of the things I liked about her was her sense of fair play. Where had her decency gone?

The idea of a house party stemmed from a desire to spend more time with Leah. Although we were neighbors, I wanted to see her more frequently to monopolize her time. Daily. Hourly.

Given my reluctance to commit to social engagements, Mother readily agreed to my proposal. Rachel practically swooned to know she would be included as a guest, able to mingle with the other adults. I'd actually enjoyed hearing Mother's detailed plans for the occasion—at least for those first two days.

After Jensen's second dismissal, my nauseated stomach should have been a clue that something was wrong. On the third day, all was confirmed. Mr. Hastings recanted and Leah stood in the window, watching me leave, a humiliated, brokenhearted fool.

Mr. Hastings's admonishment to not push, not question, to let things transpire naturally was maddening.

Mother took over preparations for the guests, and I retained the sole assignment of planning the hunts. I contemplated returning to London, but the soot-filled streets held little enticement.

Working with my steward, I threw myself into the affairs of the estate. With the help of several tenants, we repaired a long section of weatherworn fence. I assisted in the construction of a new henhouse for a young widow and commissioned repairs for the dilapidated stone wall surrounding the cemetery at the parrish.

The physical exertion occupied my body and most of my mind, but I still thought of Leah: while riding Mouse over the estate, when I saw the children run and play through the fields, and in the quiet hours of night. There were too many of those hours.

I convinced Mother to leave Riverton Park two weeks earlier than originally planned. The extra time would allow us to prepare and enjoy the estate before we were descended upon by our guests. It also allowed me to put some distance between myself and Leah.

The one upside of the house party was a confirmation by Mr. Devlin Fausett that he would attend. Fausett and I fell into an easy friendship at Cambridge. He was an interesting combination of charismatic wit and carefree panache. His visit to Landers Lodge would be most welcome.

Fausett joined me to scout out the hunting and tour the local area. I was not exactly unhappy that our outing caused us to miss the Ansleys' arrival the day before.

Today, the Hastingses were due.

I rose before the sun and employed Mouse for an early morning ride. Upon returning to the house, I bathed and dressed and watched time slowly pass, listening for the sounds of a carriage.

Finally, they arrived.

I joined Mother on the front steps to welcome the family. The carriage door opened, and I could not help the happiness seeping through my soul at the very sight of Leah. She stepped from the carriage, avoiding my gaze, but to see her in the flesh, alive and well—it made me happy.

I missed my friend. I loved my friend. I loved her. Leah. If only she felt the same.

CHAPTER 16
Miss Leah Hastings

I ASKED FOR A TRAY to be brought to my room. Surely Mr. Brumley had an ornate feast planned for the gathered party; however, two days of travel had weakened my resolve to be strong.

It had been an unexpected ray of sunlight to see Charles waiting on the stone steps. My emotions always betrayed me this way, making me feel happy when I did not wish to. I had not seen him since I stood in the window and watched him ride away, and the last time we had spoken was at his mother's dinner party.

His pleasure at our arrival was evident and made me cinch tight the happiness that threatened to break loose at the sight of his smile and coaxing eyes. Instead of watching Mr. Brumley, I admired the grandeur of the place.

Aunt Evelyn had ogled all the way up the lane. She commented on the vast property, the perfectly situated lodge, the lush forest to the east, and the quaint pond set ideally beyond the outer wall. It took a lot to impress my aunt, and Landers Lodge had done precisely that.

"Mr. Clem would have loved such a place," Aunt Evelyn gushed.

Darkened gray by time, the massive stone walls were ironically welcoming. The grand chimney was an imposing piece of architecture, but the rounded lines of the roof somehow softened its threat and transformed the lodge into a protective sort of sanctuary.

My room perfectly matched my taste, and I wondered if Mr. Brumley had selected this particular chamber for me. A coverlet of pale yellow covered the small four-poster bed, and lace-edged, white cotton curtains lined the two windows. The window boasted an ideal view of the pond and the hills rising beyond.

After a sound night's sleep, my nerves were more sedate although not completely at peace. I wore a plain blue gown and instructed Gerty to dress my hair simply. I needed only to survive the next four weeks and felt no desire to attract attention to myself.

Mr. Brumley and I were friends; we always had been. Spending a month in one another's presence was going to be simple. We would behave as indifferent acquaintances, nothing more.

I entered the breakfast room as a footman cleared several used mugs. Perhaps I had timed well and would have some solitude this morning. I enjoyed a small helping of breakfast quiche and was sipping my chocolate when voices rang from the hall.

An unfamiliar gentleman entered the room, followed by Mr. Brumley. Charles cut short whatever jovial tale he was sharing when he spied me sitting there.

"Ah, this must be the lovely lady we missed last night," the stranger said.

Mr. Brumley gave his companion a stern look and cleared his throat. "Mr. Devlin Fausett, allow me to introduce Miss Leah Hastings."

Mr. Fausett stepped near my chair, and I offered my hand. He firmly held my fingers and bowed his head over them. "Miss Leah, how do you do this fine morning?"

"I am well, Mr. Fausett. Thank you." I replaced my hand in my lap and tried to divert the gentleman's attention. "Please, don't let me keep you from breaking your fast."

The men proceeded to the sideboard while I pushed my food around my plate. Mr. Fausett was a handsome man. He stood slightly taller than Charles, and his dark ebony hair contrasted Charles's sun-tainted locks. Mr. Fausett's air commanded authority, yet the lines around his mouth led me to believe he offered his smile as often as he issued directions.

Mr. Fausett sat directly across the table from me. "Brumley tells me the two of you grew up together."

"Yes," I said. "And how are you acquainted?"

"Old Cambridge chums, I'm afraid. Brumley here has been telling me for years what great hunting is to be had at Landers Lodge." He leaned forward as if sharing a secret but whispered quite loudly, "I finally extracted an invitation from him and have come to verify the validity of his claim."

I smiled and took a bite, still averting my eyes from Mr. Brumley.

"I must confess," Mr. Fausett abruptly added at full volume while he waved his fork through the air, "that the other accounts to which Mr. Brumley has sworn have proven entirely true." Mr. Fausett smiled mischievously at Charles, who settled himself at the head of the table, two seats away, and an unwelcome formalness settled into the room.

Mr. Fausett began to feast, but Charles just watched me. It was unnerving. I'd thought I would be ready to face him, that I could manage a simple conversation about the weather or the company. I was wrong. I quickly set down my fork and pushed back my chair. Both gentlemen abruptly stood. "Please excuse me. My stomach is still unsettled from the carriage ride yesterday." I dropped my napkin on my plate and rushed from the room.

"Good heavens, Brumley! What did you do to her?" Mr. Fausett's voice followed me out the doorway.

I rushed out of the house, certain that I did not want to hear the reply.

CHAPTER 17
Mr. Charles Brumley

I EXPECTED SOME AWKWARD MOMENTS with Leah, but I did not fathom that she would ignore me completely. Yet I could not place blame solely on her, for I had said nothing either. My mind tried to formulate something, anything, but all I could hear was my heart pounding in my head and in my chest. My mind filled with words and feelings I could not audibly share.

Leah had rejected my offer. Her father claimed his retraction was at Leah's request. He said her heart was elsewhere, and again I wondered if I had pushed too far. I should have enjoyed her smiles and her teasing and waited until after our holiday to ask to court her. Perhaps if I had waited, things would be different now. Perhaps she would have spared me a few words, a simple joke, or a glimpse of her speckled eyes. Now she refused to even look at me.

How was it that she could push away from me so quickly? Did she not recall the laughter and joy we had shared? They were at the foremost of my thoughts, yet she dismissed them so easily.

The hunting would begin on the morrow, so I spent the remainder of the day ensuring all was prepared. Miss Leah did not cross my path again until dinner, where I was content to observe from afar her limited conversation with her aunt and Mr. Ansley. She continued to stubbornly refuse to make eye contact with me, while Mrs. Ansley did nothing but stare in my direction and whisper to her daughter.

I refused to acknowledge Mrs. Ansley's shrill deluge of comments. Thankfully, Mother and Fausett deflected most of her commentary. Ferrin seemed a willing conversationalist and several times attempted to bypass Mrs. Ansley and press Miss Ansley for a reply. Mrs. Ansley usually waved off the attempt and answered in her daughter's stead. Miss Ansley would blush prettily and stare at her plate; as always, she said nothing.

Shortly after dinner we joined the women in the drawing room. Leah feigned interest in a book, but I was not convinced. As the gentlemen sauntered in, I headed directly for the chair beside her. She was foolish to think she could ignore me for an entire month.

"Miss Leah," I said.

She glanced briefly at me then returned her eyes to her text. "Mr. Brumley."

"I hope you enjoyed dinner tonight." She offered a meager smile, pretending to keep her eyes fixed on her reading. "Is your room to your liking?" I asked.

"Yes, thank you." She turned a page.

"Leah," I whispered, and her head jerked up at my use of her Christian name. "I cannot take this any longer. Your silence is crushing me more than any words could. I never dreamt that asking your father's permission would alienate you from me completely, or I never would have dared. I just thought—"

She slammed the book closed, scanned the room, and finally turned her eyes to me. "Please, Mr. Brumley. Must we discuss this?" she asked in hushed tones.

Warring emotions flooded my senses as I held her gaze. Riveted in place, I never wanted to look away. I wanted to study every speckle in her eyes and know everything she was not willing to tell me. But I relented. "No, not this. But can we please discuss something?" I pleaded with a wan smile.

Leah closed her eyes for a long second. Then she blinked them open and glanced around the room again. When she saw Rachel playing cards with my mother, her face relaxed. Her eyes returned to mine for a single moment before she looked away again. "Very well, Mr. Brumley. We may talk."

"Good." A weight lifted from my lungs, finally allowing me to breathe freely. "I hope Landers Lodge is to your liking."

"There I can find no fault. Landers Lodge is magnificent. Everything one could want in a respite from the world." Her eyes darted around the various furnishings and paintings—everywhere but at me.

"I'm glad you like it," I said. "I see you even brought Admiral along."

She looked down, focusing on the book she turned over in her hands. "Not for your benefit, Mr. Brumley." Her eyes quickly swept my face before she returned them to her lap. She looked at me through her lashes. "Father insists Admiral is the best hunter he's ever had, despite his breeding to the contrary."

I studied her profile. "Actually I've heard of several cur that have been trained to be successful hunters. Breed has nothing to do with it. Devotion is what matters, and devotion comes from the heart not the bloodline."

Miss Leah whipped her head up and studied me intently. Something simmered there in her eyes. "Do you really believe that, Mr. Brumley? Do you believe devotion comes from the heart?"

"I do." What had caused this sudden turn of attention?

Her face remained steady, but her hands began to tangle together over the book in her lap. "And what about when it comes to society? Do you feel rank and honor have no place? Are you able to, as you say, 'Look upon the heart rather than bloodline'?"

"Honor will always have a place. A good dog is forever honorable, loyal, and devoted to his master." Ah, there was her waggling foot. I was glad to see some emotion stirring inside the passive countenance she tried to project.

"Do you think there could be loyalty even if honor is lacking?" she asked. Her eyes ignited, holding me in their trance.

I longed to uncover the passions stewing behind her burning gaze and slowly gave her my response. "I believe loyalty and honor complement one another." I reached over and placed my hand on hers, stilling her restless fingers. "Dear Leah, we are no longer talking about Admiral. What is this about?"

She swallowed, pulled her hands free from mine, and looked away as Fausett approached. Drat his interruption!

"Miss Leah, Miss Brumley has agreed to play for us, and Miss Ansley has been persuaded to sing," Fausett said.

I scoffed. "By her mother, no doubt." My fingers massaged my temple in anticipation of the flowing compliments Mrs. Ansley would soon accost us with on her daughter's behalf.

Fausett eyed me but ignored my comment. He returned his attention to Leah. "Do you sing as well? Perhaps we could have a duet?"

Leah looked over my shoulder, and her posture tensed. "Very ill, I'm afraid," she said softly. She placed the book on the table to her right and stood. "If you will excuse me, gentlemen. I am going to retire for the evening. Please give my excuses to Rachel." She glanced over my shoulder again and, with a stiff smile, added, "And to Miss Ansley, of course."

With that, she scurried from the room, and I received another disparaging look from Fausett.

CHAPTER 18
Miss Leah Hastings

❧❀❧

IN AN EFFORT TO AVOID Charles—and Mrs. Ansley—I had taken a nap earlier in the afternoon. So I was not truly tired. However, I did not wish to continue my conversation with Mr. Brumley nor endure the constant barrage of silent reprimands from that particular lady.

Mr. Brumley contended that honor and loyalty were intertwined. If Mrs. Ansley followed through on her threat to disgrace my family, would Charles abandon us? Would he abandon me? He could not know of Mrs. Ansley's blackmail, for he would surely try to find a solution, and that was a course I could not let him pursue. Her threat was real and valid. I had seen Father dismiss Louisa's pleadings. He could have sent for the doctor, but he didn't. If I ignored Mrs. Ansley, she would expose the truth, despoil our family name, and bring shame upon the Hastings household. It was a chance I could not take.

Charles and I could not wed, but would he still befriend me, or would I lose him as a confidant as well? I laughed sadly at the realization that it had already happened. I already could not confide my darkest fear to Charles. Mrs. Ansley had effectively separated us.

My hostility towards Charles was uncalled for. He had been a competent and obliging host thus far—except for the fact that he could read me so easily. He knew when I was ruffled and was not afraid to question me about my shifting temperament. Perhaps what riled me was his assumption that I wanted to talk to him. And the fact that he was right.

I dismissed Gerty once I was in my nightdress, but I had no inclination towards sleep. I cracked the window to let the cool night seep in. After pacing the room a dozen times, I fell back onto my bed. Why did I feel so disconcerted?

Landers Lodge was beautiful. The weather had held unseasonably warm. I was familiar with all individuals present, notwithstanding my new acquaintance, Mr. Fausett, who had proved quite amiable. I threw my arms over my face.

Devotion comes from the heart, Mr. Brumley had said. For nineteen years I had devoted my life to him. My devotion had flowed through every vein of my being and ebbed through my heart. It had not been enough. If Charles's devotion had been equivalent, things would be different now. We would be wed, and Mrs. Ansley would have no reason to threaten me or my family.

Yet, I could not erase his words from my mind. *Loyalty and honor complement one another.*

A frustrated growl escaped my throat. I would never figure out that man! His words were a constant contradiction of his actions. I did not believe such a deep-seated conviction could be new, but if he had felt that way one year ago, it would mean that his feelings remained unchanged. If he dismissed my sentiments and walked away a year ago, why now was he wishing to court me? Why, now that it was impossible, did he want to pursue a relationship?

After seeing his happy expression upon our arrival, I believed maybe Charles did feel some sort of tendresse for me. Had he one year ago? In that instant, I had allowed a tiny moment of wonder, a flicker of possibility. But what Charles felt one year ago no longer mattered. Nor did what either of us felt now. The flame was smothered before it could ignite into something viable and real. Mrs. Ansley's threat ensured it was doused completely. If only I could make my heart acknowledge that fact.

I did not move. I tried not to think or feel or dream. I concentrated on breathing, in and out, waiting for night to pass and another wearisome day to arrive.

CHAPTER 19
Mr. Charles Brumley

Ꙩ

AFTER A RESTLESS NIGHT, I rose early to finalize preparations for the hunt. Ferrin was already at breakfast.

"Good morning, Brumley," he said with far too much cheer.

"Is it? I hadn't noticed yet," I replied dryly.

Ferrin eyed me as I dished my food. "Everything all right?"

I shot him a glare and crumpled into my seat.

"Might this have anything to do with a particular sister of mine?" He chuckled and leaned back, crossing his legs. "Or perhaps your mood has something to do with a pressing mother and her fair-eyed daughter?"

I tossed my toast onto my plate. "We used to spend entire afternoons together, and now she refuses to even talk to me! And Mrs. Ansley?" My jaw clenched, and I shook my head. After releasing a heavy breath, I continued. "Mother insisted we invite them. What am I to do?"

Ferrin raised his hands in defense. "Don't look at me, old chap. I've yet to understand the fairer sex." His laugh quieted, and he sat thoughtfully for a moment. "In the first case, perhaps you need to consider what has changed." I looked at him quizzically. "If you and Leah used to get on well and now you don't, what happened?" He stood and moved behind his chair. Gripping the spindles, he slid the seat under the edge of the table. "And in the second case, maybe the fair-eyed beauty needs a handsome distraction." He pumped his eyebrows and grinned then excused himself, leaving me to my thoughts.

What had happened with Leah? I knew the answer.

I had attended far too many routs with assuming, brash females. I had skirted conversations suggesting marriage, courting, future plans, and even one Miss Benedict, who wanted to begin discussing offspring. The marriage mart was painful, to be sure, and I did not mind offering a rejection to the arduous, presumptive ladies. I wanted more in a wife, more in a marriage.

My parents had got on well. They loved their children, and my upbringing was agreeable and generally happy. My desire was to settle for nothing less. I did not mind dismissing the eligible ladies of the ton, who looked only upon my holdings and my inheritance.

But there was one dismissal for which I could claim regret, and that was Leah. For years she had trusted me and confided in me. On that perfect summer day, I had enjoyed her company immensely. Then when she confessed her deepest of feelings, when she revealed her heart, I cowardly pulled away, turned tail, and ran.

The truth hit me then. It was no wonder she had no desire to talk about anything beyond the weather. So many other women had persisted despite numerous hints and slights. Leah was resilient in so many things, but when I told her no, when I rejected her heart, she took me to my word. What a blasted fool I was!

I had to win her back. Yet how was I to do that when she wouldn't even talk to me? Could everything we'd shared be lost? I didn't know if I was fighting to win her again or if I was fighting to win her back. Mr. Hastings's explanation had been vague at best. Had Captain Wilkins won my Leah's heart?

For Mrs. Ansley's part, I agreed with Ferrin's assertion that a distraction was in order. It seemed he was willing to step into that role, or perhaps I could enlist Fausett's help. Either way, as far as Miss Ansley was concerned, it was time to call in a favor.

Between the five men, our total bag for the first day was ninety-eight birds. On our second day we improved our accuracy and shot a bag of 132.

The hunts provided a much-needed diversion. Over dinner we bragged to the ladies, embellished our stories, and upped the numbers. My efforts to engage Leah in conversation failed again and again. She was civil towards me, nothing more.

After a restless night, I made my way to the stables, determined that a brisk ride in the morning air would help clear the cobwebs that constantly clouded my mind and played with my emotions. As I neared the stables, I heard a voice within. It was one I knew well.

"There now. You are a beautiful beast," Leah cooed softly.

I peeked around the barn door to see her forehead pressed against Mouse's nuzzle. Her curls hung loose down her back, and her coat was wrapped tightly around her. My heart warmed, and I didn't breathe for fear that the moment would end.

"Does Charles take good care of you?" she asked. "Does he make you laugh? Does he tease you relentlessly?" Her hand caressed Mouse's nose. "Or does he drive you mad with confusion?"

My peaceful reverie was shaken. The serenity I felt fissured like a giant crevasse. I shifted, and Leah turned towards me. She did not seem alarmed by my presence. Did she know I had been eavesdropping?

"Mr. Brumley," Leah said. "Mouse and I were just talking about you."

"So I heard."

"You did?" Her arms wrapped around her waist, and we both watched the toe of her boot draw circles in the dirt. She didn't know I had been there.

I stepped closer. Her nose and cheeks were tinted pink from the brisk morning. "Mad with confusion?" I asked.

"'Tis nothing, Mr. Brumley. Mouse and I were just . . ."

". . . comparing notes," I finished for her.

She stomped her feet, squared her shoulders, and raised her eyes to mine. "Yes, well. Enjoy your ride." Leah brushed past me as if the conversation were over.

It was not.

I turned and matched her movement as she walked past. "Mad with confusion, Leah? What does that mean?" I pressed.

Her coat swung around her waist as she faced me again. "It means, Mr. Brumley, that you are maddening and confusing all at the same time."

"Is that even possible?" I asked, although I knew the feeling well and true.

Leah turned to look at my horse and then turned back to me with a definitive nod. "Mouse and I both agree that not many people could pull it off. But yes, you have succeeded in accomplishing both."

"A compliment, then?" I asked, hoping to pull the conversation to lighter topics. She'd finally spoken more than a single sentence, and I yearned for more. But the wrath in her eyes confirmed it was not to be.

"Hardly." She stood still for a moment, the moisture pooling in her eyes. Then she turned abruptly and walked out of the barn.

A week into our holiday, I extended an invitation to some of our neighbors to join in the sport and remain for a picnic. Mr. Wood and his wife, my nearest neighbors, joined us, along with Colonel Allen, with whom I had made an acquaintance several years before.

On that particular morning, birds were sparse, perhaps having fled after our previous two outings. I instructed my men to gather the downed fowl, and we retired to a small grove of trees near the pond. The day was ideal. A light breeze chased away any unpleasantness and allowed the sunshine to brighten and cheer.

A lavish spread of cold meats, cheese, hard bread, and fresh fruit awaited our delight in the shade. I offered my compliments to Mrs. June and asked her to pass on my gratitude to Mrs. Rowe. I turned to see the ladies approaching from the house.

Leah greeted her father with a kiss and offered a sincere acknowledgment to Mr. Fausett. His reaction to the attentions she would not spare me did not disappoint. He removed his hat with a flourish and nearly doubled over into a low bow. Miss Leah giggled softly then turned back to her father. "How was your sport today?" she asked.

"Fine, fine." Mr. Hastings waved off her question. "The birds all seemed to be hiding. Did they not, Brumley?"

"Yes, sir. I think your fine shooting has scared them off." I motioned the ladies towards the food. "Mother, won't you please start us off?"

Rachel stepped behind Mrs. Wood and turned around to address Leah. "I've heard it has become fashionable for women to shoot with the men. What do you make of it, Miss Leah?"

Mrs. Clem harrumphed her disapproval and began filling her plate.

Miss Leah smiled at her aunt then turned to Rachel. "I've never much cared for guns. However, I wouldn't mind learning to shoot a bow."

"I would be honored to be your instructor in archery, Miss Leah," Fausett offered. He stood near the ladies and flashed his bright smile. "I find I like the sport rather well. For so many goals, the end result is obtuse. Fishing, for example, requires an inordinate amount of patience, an area where I find myself lacking. Fencing requires skill, yet is also dependent on your opponent. Archery can be mastered individually and is all about precision. Either you hit the target or you do not."

Leah turned back towards the table. "I appreciate the offer, sir, but I would not wish to distract from your time here."

"It would be a most welcome diversion," he replied with a tilt of his head.

Rachel giggled as I sent a frosty glare at my friend.

"A woman should know her place," Mrs. Ansley said haughtily. "A lady's time would be much better spent improving her skills in music, the arts, or language. To desire to pursue a man's sport! It's unfathomable. My Catherine would never be found in such a masculine pursuit."

Miss Ansley's voice rang sweet and soft. "I've read of many archery clubs in Town where the women participate alongside the gentlemen. I think archery would not be entirely unsuitable."

"But guns!" Mrs. Ansley's voice sounded especially brash compared to Miss Ansley's more tempered tone. "No proper female would even consider such a thing."

Poor Rachel. Her cheeks blazed red from Mrs. Ansley's rebuke. With her head hung, she sat near my mother on the blanket and stared at her plate.

"I disagree," Leah said. Mrs. Ansley rolled her eyes and scowled, but Leah continued. "I believe it's important to discuss such matters. I am not saying I'm in favor of women hunting, but it was not long ago that women were forced into marriage contracts. I welcome discussions and the changes they bring." Leah offered a sympathetic glance to Rachel.

Mrs. Ansley turned to fill her plate. Leah frowned at the woman's back and then moved to sit as far away from me as possible. My stomach tightened, both at Mrs. Ansley's slight to my sister and Leah's aloofness. My appetite fled.

Colonel Allen piled his plate high and remarked, "I agree that guns can be intimidating, yet in my profession pistols and swordplay are skills we must master."

"I know a chap," Ferrin said, waving his fork through the air. "Perhaps you have had occasion to meet him? Robert Wilkins? He was recently commissioned a captain in the Second Division of the Fifty-Second Infantry." He leaned casually back on his elbows and threw out Captain Wilkins's name as if they were old schoolmates.

Leah clamped her mouth shut and chewed. She must have swallowed hastily, for she began to choke. Leah placed a hand on her neck as if she could will the coughing to stop. Her throat would not calm its convulsions, and she continued to hack while her cheeks burned crimson.

"Miss Leah, are you quite all right?" my mother asked.

Her eyes began to water as she attempted to wave off any concern. Stubborn girl!

Retrieving a glass of water, I knelt beside her. Leah accepted my offer, and the cool water soothed her cough.

"That is much better, thank you." She took another drink and raised her eyes to mine.

I pulled out my handkerchief and reached over to wipe the tears from her face. Leah held me in a trance as my finger slowly caressed her cheek through the linen. My heart quickened, and I watched a few more tears trail down.

"Are you sure you are all right?" I asked softly, offering my handkerchief to her.

The remainder of the guests blended into obscurity. It was simply Leah and me, the way I had imagined so many times since my epiphany on that summer day long ago. This moment resembled the way we had been, the way we should be. I wanted to move closer, to touch her face again, to feel the warmth and tenderness I saw radiating from her eyes as they searched my face. I leaned forward, slowly, until Mr. Hastings's voice sliced through the moment.

"Leah, are you sure you're recovered?" he asked.

Leah blinked, and the spell was broken. "Yes, I believe so," she said. Then her eyes narrowed, and she whispered, "But I am not entirely sure."

The defenses in which Miss Leah had ensconced herself somehow fell. The conversation at the picnic had seemed to widen the divide between us. Then, with the offer of water, a sublime caress—everything changed. When I brushed her skin, lightning shot up my arm and throughout my entire being. Surely, this sensation was too strong to be felt by me alone.

"Could I convince you to join me for a short stroll towards the pond to regain your composure?" I asked.

"Yes, I think I would like that."

She stood, straightened her skirts, and accepted my proffered arm. We remained within view of her father, but I purposefully led her to the far side of the water and out of earshot of the others.

We walked in silence, Miss Leah focusing on the ground. I focused on her profile. More specifically, I focused on her soft lashes, perfectly tipped nose, and sweet lips. I closed my eyes for a moment, unsure of where to start. I could not continue to look at her and restrain myself. Every time her eyes avoided mine or she smiled at everyone except me or she sat as far away as possible, it felt like dismissal all over again. I was not strong enough to survive her rejection many more times, not when we shared moments as sacred as this.

I cleared my throat. "Miss Leah, I know you asked me not to broach the subject, but . . . um . . . well . . ."

Leah stopped and laid her hand on my arm. "I was wrong to put you off, Charles. There are reasons, ones that I am unable to change. I hope one day you will forgive me."

Reasons she could not change? Would a change in reason mean a change in her heart? It was not much, but it was a start. I placed my free hand upon hers. "There will always be room in my heart for you, dear Leah."

The walls instantly began to rise again. She tensed, and when I looked at her eyes I saw sorrow, fear, longing—all raging a battle inside. She was trying to parry them all—to push her defenses down or build them up? I was not sure. "What is this demon keeping you from me?" I asked.

Leah looked away. "I'm sorry, Charles. I can't."

"Can't or won't?" I pleaded.

"Both." She looked at me, the battle in her eyes decided. The walls had been restored.

"Does this have to do with Captain Wilkins?"

Her mouth began to open in response, but she slowly closed it.

My pulse quickened. "Does he . . . are you . . . in love with him?" My voice was clipped and sharp.

"I . . ." Leah struggled to find the words she wanted. Her eyes were scared, and I wanted to pull her close and tell her it would be okay. But it wouldn't. She wanted another. She had chosen not to be *my* Leah but *his*.

"Forgive me for meddling; it's not my affair." After a quick bow, I retreated with my heartache to the house.

CHAPTER 20
Miss Leah Hastings

❧❦❧

THE PREVIOUS DAYS OF HUNTING had taken the gentlemen to the far edges of the estate, but today they were to shoot nearer to the house. Mr. Brumley had planned two more days of sport over the following week and then a ball a few days later to cap off the festivities.

We completed breakfast, and the women gathered on the vestibule to send the men off. Father was checking his fowling piece, and Admiral ran over to greet me. My fingers instinctively reached down to pet his lusciously soft fur.

"I see you and Admiral still share a rapport." Charles walked up with his weapon shouldered.

We had not spoken since the previous day. When Ferrin asked Colonel Allen about Captain Wilkins, the question caught me off guard. Charles came to my rescue with a glass of water and his reassuring touch. My jostled emotions were too fresh to discuss.

For a moment, our relationship was exactly as I remembered: Charles and I talking, sharing, and opening up to each other. Then he asked the one thing I could not share. He believed my refusal was related to Captain Wilkins. No one could know the real culprit was Mrs. Ansley.

"Brumley!" Father shouted. "We shall enjoy the ladies' company soon enough. Come, man."

"It seems you are needed, Mr. Brumley." I nodded towards the group awaiting their host.

"I do hope so, Miss Leah, for it is a marvelous feeling indeed to be needed." Charles stood unmoving, his eyes drawn and distant.

Mrs. Ansley coughed forcibly behind me.

Then Catherine's soft voice canceled her mother's harshness. "Best of luck, Mr. Brumley." A second later she added, "And you also, Mr. Hastings."

Ferrin turned around with a large grin, touched his hat, and then called Admiral to his side. Charles looked between Ferrin and Miss Ansley, and I thought I spied a small smirk as he turned to join the others. I pulled my coat tight, wrapped my arms around my middle, and watched their retreating figures until the men rounded the rushes at the far end of the pond.

Mrs. Brumley led the women back to the house, but I did not follow. Instead I wandered through the garden, needing the tranquility of the cool, sharp air. The blooms were fading this far into fall. Only a few colorful flowers held their heads high and proud.

After a deep breath, Mr. Brumley's grinning face entered my mind, and my heartbeat quickened. He wanted to be needed. I *had* needed him, and he deserted me. Had the roles reversed? Would I desert him? Did I have any alternative?

There felt such a great division between needs and wants. Why must the two be locked in constant battle? Would there ever be a time when they would be one and the same? There must be some measure of desire, for Charles had asked to court me. I assumed it was partially because we were well suited, despite the incessant teasing. Yet to be needed inferred something more. An object not only desired but essential. Was I essential to Charles, or was I simply another game, a pastime until a better diversion came along?

My mind was so very confused. Walking among the barren hedge no longer pacified me. My legs, my head, indeed my entire core, yearned for more. Scanning my surroundings, I saw a maid washing the windows inside the library. I crossed to the edge of the gardens, where she could no longer see me, and stepped off the path. Then I lifted my skirts and ran.

To feel so light, so free, feelings I had lost hope of experiencing again. My hem became damp from the morning dew, but I did not care. I ran and breathed, the burning in my lungs transforming my stagnant heart to one that felt. It ached and pounded and screamed for freedom. If only I could feel this burning constantly. Like the rejuvenating fire of a phoenix, I felt new.

The rushes near the pond marked the end of my regeneration. Over my labored breath, I heard a few shots and a dog barking. Then came the distant voices of the men, and I realized I may not have chosen the safest destination.

When I turned back towards the lodge, another volley of shots rang out. I spun around and walked backwards. Shielding the sun from my eyes, I tried to spot the fowl the men were aiming for.

Silence filled the air—until the shouting began.

A servant broke from the tall grass of the pond and sprinted towards the stable yelling for a horse to be saddled. His face was pale, and my eyes fell to the bright crimson stain on his coat.

Fear clenched my gut. I looked back at the pond and saw the gentlemen scrambling towards the house. Mr. Fausett and Ferrin were the last to step into view. They carried a limp body between them. My heart stopped when I recognized that the unmoving man was my father.

CHAPTER 21
Mr. Charles Brumley

❧✦❧

THE BEATERS DROVE THE FOWL towards our line, and Craig, our gamekeeper, held us at the ready. Finally, Craig gave the go-ahead. Singling out my target, I pulled the trigger just as the bird fell into a dive. I took aim again, following the line, but Admiral began to bark, effectively breaking my concentration.

I lowered my fowling piece to my side. "What is it, Admiral?"

He danced around haphazardly, right and left. I brushed off his antics, assuming he was anxious to go collect the bounty. Several more shots sounded as Ferrin and Colonel Allen found their marks.

Another bird launched from the grass, and I raised my weapon. My finger held steady on the trigger, waiting for the perfect shot. There it was. My finger pulled, and suddenly I found myself on my back with the shot reverberating in my ear. The wind was knocked from my lungs as Admiral's large paws pinned me down.

Shouts rang above me, and commotion ensued. I shoved the dog away and pushed myself up. My insides lurched at the scene before me. A servant rolled Mr. Hastings on to his back. Blood began to saturate his coat just below his left shoulder. The servant stepped aside to allow Ferrin a closer view. Ferrin leaned over his father and began to shout orders.

"It's bad, sir," the servant said to me, his face white and his shirt saturated with blood.

"Quick, lad, fetch the doctor," Fausett directed as he stepped up beside me and pulled me to my feet. The young boy ran through the rushes calling for a horse.

Colonel Allen shook off his jacket and folded it into a haphazard square. He knelt beside Ferrin. "We must staunch the bleeding," Colonel

Allen said, pressing his coat against Mr. Hastings's shoulder. He turned back to Ferrin. "What happened, man?"

Ferrin lifted his eyes from his father and turned their burning fury on me. "Brumley!" he spat.

My mouth fell open to form an explanation that did not come. Ferrin's fist connected with my jaw, and I staggered sideways.

"Hastings!" Fausett spoke sharply. "Not now. We must get your father to the house."

Ferrin's eyes glazed cold as he suppressed the fire inside. He turned and walked to his father, who moaned in pain. Colonel Allen held the coat firmly and helped raise Mr. Hastings forward. Ferrin slipped his hands under his father's arms, and Fausett lifted Mr. Hastings's feet. They began the slow procession towards the house while Colonel Allen applied pressure to the wound.

I followed numbly behind and massaged my jaw. What had happened? I was aiming at the bird, but Admiral—he jumped and the volley was sent.

We cleared the rushes, and the house came into view. The details would have to be settled later. Right now we needed to tend to Mr. Hastings. My senses awakened, and I began to jog towards the house.

"Father!"

I turned and saw Leah running to meet us. I looked between her and Ferrin. No words were spoken, but volumes of understanding passed between them. Ferrin's eyes were hard and filled with disgust. Leah saw his derision, his loathing anger. She turned towards me, and I opened my mouth to explain.

"Charles?" she pled.

With one word, she was asking so much. My mouth clamped closed. I shook my head once and ran to the house.

CHAPTER 22
Miss Leah Hastings

છ૭૱૭૭

I PRESSED THE DAMP CLOTH to Father's head and watched his shallow breathing. Another tear fell.

"Miss Leah, are you sure you wouldn't like Mrs. June to take a watch?" the doctor asked.

I adamantly shook my head and wiped my face free of the tears that would not cease. "I need to be here."

He nodded in understanding. "Very well. I shall take some refreshment and return shortly." He stepped from the room.

Ferrin stared out the library window, his hand propped against the wall, bracing him from unleashing the wrath that had been compounding for the past hour.

"He retrieved the bullet; that must be something," I said softly, hoping that if I verbalized my wish, it would be granted.

"Leah," Ferrin chastised, "you heard the doctor. Father is not expected to last the night."

My chest tightened again. Fear grasped my lungs and refused to release. Words felt futile, but I said them anyway. "Perhaps he is wrong." I stroked Father's soft hair.

Aunt Evelyn had never dealt well in the sickroom. At the first sight of Father, she fainted. Mr. Ansley had been kind enough to see her to her room, and there she remained. I was surprised, though, that Charles had not come.

I asked Ferrin, "Where is Mr. Brumley? I thought he would at least check to see that our needs were met."

"I asked him to let us mourn in solitude."

Next to Aunt Evelyn, the Brumleys were the closest thing we had to family. I wondered why Ferrin would dismiss Charles. He must have seen the question in my eyes.

"Dear Leah." Ferrin rounded the couch to hold me in a hug that I desperately needed.

"What happened?" I asked, sobbing into Ferrin's shirt.

Ferrin's arms stiffened, and I pulled my head back to look up at him. He would not meet my gaze; instead he looked over the top of my head and out the window. His eyes were filled with tears that would escape if he allowed them to.

I wiped my cheeks clear of my tears and reigned in my emotions. I had to be strong for Father. He was not gone yet, and I refused to surrender. My brother's mouth pinched closed, and his jaw flexed tight. "Ferrin?"

Surely it was an accident. Whose gun had discharged? Was one of the servants to blame? Or was it a faulty weapon? Was it Father's fowling piece? Ferrin knew, and the longer he delayed, the more curious I became.

He slowly shook his head. "Now is not the time, Leah. Now we must concentrate on Father. Everything else will be dealt with . . . in time."

CHAPTER 23
Mr. Charles Brumley

ᴄᴏᴢᴄᴏ

Mʏ ᴘᴀᴄɪɴɢ ᴡᴀs ᴡᴇᴀʀɪɴɢ ᴛʜᴇ carpet bare, but I could not stop moving. If I stopped, I had to face reality. If I stopped, I had to acknowledge what had happened. Pacing was mindless. In a way, the constant motion kept me grounded, yet it did nothing to ease the whirlwind inside.

A rap on the door altered my direction, and I walked over to open it.

"Can I ring for some tea?" Fausett asked as he stepped inside. "You haven't had any refreshment since breakfast, and this promises to be a long night."

I walked back around the far side of my book room and braced my arms on the desk. "I can't reconcile it," I said. "What caused the dog to jump? One moment I was aiming at a pheasant, and the next I had shot the poor man." I hung my head in despair.

"Have you had a chance to speak with Ferrin?" Fausett asked.

"Not since the facer he landed me." My jaw still hurt from the well-deserved hit. "Ferrin asked me to clear out."

"Leah? Have you spoken with her?"

I shook my head. "Ha!" came the strangled cry. "It's no use. Once she knows it was my weapon, she will never speak to me again." I motioned to the door. "It's too much. There's no hope now." My fist slammed down on the desk.

Fausett reached for the door handle. "It was an accident, Brumley. Give it time," he said and left the room.

Time was what I feared. The next moment could be Mr. Hastings's last. The next moment could seal my fate as the guilty party who killed the father of the woman I loved.

It was true that time could also prove kind, bestowing one more hour or one more day. However, I could not be satisfied with either finite limitation for I wanted a lifetime, and my only hope for eternity was for Mr. Hastings to first survive the night. I hung my head again, and as the clock on the mantel chimed the hour, I began to pray.

CHAPTER 24
Miss Leah Hastings

❧

MY EYES BLINKED OPEN, AND I realized I had fallen asleep slumped over the side of Father's bed. I still held his hand in mine as sunlight peeked through the curtains and signaled the new morning. The events of the previous day crowded my mind, flashing again and again through my memory. Father's chest slowly rose. He exhaled and drew another breath.

He had survived the night. It was the first step in a miracle, and a tiny seed of hope blossomed within me.

Then, as if Father wanted to sour my optimism, he took three or four short, ragged breaths, and I panicked at the sound of him painfully sucking in the air. Finally, his chest fell back into a steady, slow rhythm, and he slept on.

Ferrin had collapsed in an armchair on the opposite side of the bed. He continued to sleep as well. My grip on Father's hand loosened. A curl fell across my face, and I realized what an unkempt mess I had become. It would be an easy thing to wash up then return to attend Father. I backed into the hall and quietly pulled the door shut. There was a shuffling behind me, and I turned to see Charles hunched over in a chair across from the door. He looked awful. "Have you been here all night?" I asked.

His dark-rimmed eyes answered my inquiry. "I wanted to be here in case . . . in case you needed anything." I felt certain he had been about to say something else.

My eyes narrowed. "You could have asked a servant to wait."

"It's my—" Charles paused, looking worn and beaten, like he'd wandered straight from a battle but was still uncertain of the outcome. He debated what he wanted to say; then his mouth turned down. "It's my responsibility." He stood and wiped his hand over his face. "How is he, Leah?"

Charles's eyes mirrored my sorrow. My focus was on Father. None of my other walls mattered at that moment. Charles was the host, and we were his responsibility. I hadn't considered the ramifications of Father being hurt at Landers Lodge. Charles respected my father, and his concern was evident in his unshaven face and bloodshot eyes.

"He is alive." I choked on the words and raised a hand to my mouth. Once I had steadied myself, I continued. "He's sleeping, and his breathing appears to be fairly steady. The doctor gave him plenty of laudanum, so I pray he will continue to rest this morning until the doctor returns."

"And—and how are you?" Charles took a tentative step towards me.

His words touched me more than they should have. My attention wandered around the hall, avoiding his gaze. I refused to look directly at Charles, because if I did, I would see something I was not ready for—empathy. His voice was laden with it. "I will continue to hope for the best," I said.

"If only optimism were a balm. You ever were the optimist."

At this, my eyes met his, and he offered a meager smile. Fatigue tried my patience. I wanted to respond with some snide remark. I wanted to remind Charles that my optimism drove him away—

Wait. Did that mean I had driven him away? Was I to blame for him running? I always assumed it was bachelorhood he wanted, yet after our conversation near the stables, I realized I had never heard anything that would sully Charles's reputation. He had remained an upstanding gentleman. His time in London was not spent cavorting with woman or gambling or anything scandalous. In fact, I knew very little of his life in the last year. I begrudged him leaving and placed the blame on him. Did part of that blame fall to me as well?

Exhaustion shook my frame, and I staggered to regain my balance. I braced a hand against the wall, and Charles stepped forward to assist me.

"Whoa, I've got you." His warm breath brushed my ear.

His hand wrapped around my waist and held me firmly. Charles's touch was so welcome that I turned into him then gasped when I realized my hands were resting on his chest. I stared at his crumpled cravat and was grateful he was holding me upright. My heart beat rapidly, most assuredly from my fatigue and the unexpected closeness. He was so very close and so very warm.

After a long minute and a few stabilizing breaths, I had composed myself enough to rely on the merit of my own legs. My hands slid from

Charles's chest up to his shoulders, and I looked up at him to tell him that I was okay.

His tired eyes examined me intently. His gaze searched my face in a silence that was not at all comfortable. I was tongue-tied and weary and churning with uncertainty.

Charles's eyes stopped dancing around my face and settled on my mouth. I inhaled quickly and closed my lips. He leaned forward slowly, and I did not react—beyond curling my fingers around his lapels. But when my somnolent mind awakened to the yearning in his eyes, I yelped and jumped backward like a startled child.

My breaths came quick and heavy, and I stared at his forlorn expression as he stepped back. Charles would have kissed me. I lifted my fingers to my mouth and covered my quivering stomach with my other arm.

He closed his eyes briefly and stepped back against the wall. "I'm sorry."

As I examined his face, the look I saw there frightened me. Charles was weary, but his eyes told me he was cognizant of everything that had just passed between us. His determination, his desire, his strength—I saw it all and knew I could not remain. I scurried away and heard him whisper again, "I'm sorry."

At the bottom of the staircase, I paused. Resting my hand on the banister, I glanced back at Charles. What could he have to be sorry for? Was he sorry he almost kissed me? He stared at me with so much sorrow it made me ache. My free hand had to grasp my chest to make sure my heart would not burst from within me.

"Good morning, Miss Leah. How is your father?" I jerked around and saw Catherine descending the stairs.

It took a moment for me to register the question she asked. I slowly blinked and tried to focus. Then I replied, "He is still breathing, Miss Ansley. Please forgive me." I turned and fled to my room.

CHAPTER 25
Mr. Charles Brumley

❧

LEAH'S REJECTION DID NOT STING as much as her pity. She did not know of my part in the accident; that was the only explanation for it. I had waited outside the library all night, dreading the cries I would hear if her father passed. Sleep had been a ghost, teasing and haunting me through the endless hours of darkness. It was all I could do to push the invented horror away and focus on reality. I listened intently for any sound escaping the library; I hoped every second for another quiet breath and then another. They continued to build, one upon the next, until the light began to dissipate the darkness.

Gentle, welcome sunlight flooded into the entryway at the end of the hall. The shadows began to flee, and then Leah emerged like golden sunshine.

I knew it would come, illumination. First the morning light and eventually the truth. Leah would find out.

Holding her so close, so perfectly in my arms, my mind gave way to my heart, and I had almost kissed her. She had to know what I was about to do. I took solace in the fact that she did not berate me for my actions. She simply pushed me away and left. I had been on the receiving end of Leah's temper enough to know that were she truly irate, there would have been a much stronger rebuke. Once she had rested and broken her fast, it may still come. I would enjoy the lull in the storm while I could.

My desire for her to know my part in her father's accident was unequivocally linked to my desire that she never find out. I wanted Leah forever, and there was no way to keep a secret like this. Not if I truly loved her.

Every moment I waited, wondering if she knew, was the most extreme torture I had ever experienced—twisting and kicking and thwarting my spirit. I believed it would be best to face the guillotine once rather than wait for the moment of exile again and again and again. I would tell her. Soon.

I bathed quickly, shaved, and put on a clean change of clothes; when I jogged back down the stairs, the doctor stood in the drawing room giving Mother an update.

"All of Mr. Hastings's vitals appear stable. His breathing is more shallow than I would like, but it's steady, which is a good sign. I will return again tomorrow unless a change requires my presence sooner. Please do not hesitate to call for me again."

"Thank you, Doctor." Mother stood, and they walked to the door.

I acknowledged them as they passed. Mother gave me a heavy, weighted look, a combination of doubt, hope, fear, and the strangled knowledge that it was all out of our control. I envied Leah and her optimism.

Leah! I wondered if she had seen the doctor and heard his prognosis. I walked towards the library, and as I rounded the corner, I saw her slip out the back entrance of the house.

I followed, watching as she dragged her right hand behind her, brushing lightly over the tops of the shrubs. I quietly trailed behind, considering how to approach her.

She must have felt my eyes on her back because she suddenly spun around. "Mr. Brumley," she said on a whisper.

I held my breath. Tracks of tears ran down her cheeks. She didn't even bother to wipe them away. She looked at me as if the next moment would splinter her into a thousand pieces. My heart ached and clenched so hard I didn't think I would be able to stand much longer. I widened my stance, bracing myself for the hit.

"Did you hear?" Leah's voice sang, catching me off guard. "The doctor thinks Father will recover." Her face split into a smile. My limbs froze. Had Ferrin not yet unveiled the truth? She walked towards me, warming my soul with each step. "Thank you, Charles."

Charles? No, no, no! This was all wrong. "Why are you thanking me?" I cried out. I had to tell her.

"Did you not say my optimism was a balm?" She was too close now. She reached out with her bare fingers and grabbed my hands, clutching them in her own.

"No, Leah." I shook my head. This could not go on.

"It worked. Father is recovering. The doctor said! And soon he will be better and—"

"Leah!" I said fiercely, squeezing her hands in mine. She stopped talking.

She tilted her head, and her smile began to melt away. "What is it, Charles? Has Father opened his eyes?" There was a hope in her voice that shattered my heart.

"There is no change. Your father is just as the doctor left him."

Her smile returned. "And isn't that good news?" She moved a hand to my arm.

I closed my eyes and tilted my head towards the sun. "Oh, Leah! I have to tell you."

She pulled her hands free and let them fall to her side. "Tell me what?" Her voice caught with innocence.

"Leah!" Ferrin shouted and ran to where we stood. He looked between us, his jaw tense. Finally he said, "Come quickly! Father is awake!"

Leah's face lit up once more. She pushed up on her toes, kissed my cheek, lifted her skirts, and ran inside.

Ferrin stood with his chest heaving. The furious storm in his eyes threatened to lash out. "I thought I asked you to leave us alone."

"I have to tell her what happened." My chin notched up a few degrees. "She ought to hear it from me."

Ferrin's shoulders rose, and he gave a single nod. "Very well. But wait until Father is out of danger. She shouldn't have to deal with losing two men she loves at once."

Two men?

"Ferrin, do you mean to say . . ."

One look from Ferrin cut off my question. "What *was* no longer matters, Brumley. There is only what *is*." Ferrin swept back inside.

He was right. Reality was truth, and the truth was all that mattered. There was no more dreaming or pretending. Leah would soon know the truth, my part in the accident. She would know and have nothing to do with me. Ever.

I rushed to the stables and prepared my horse. I needed to ride far away from this place.

CHAPTER 26
Miss Leah Hastings

❦

FATHER IMPROVED EVERY DAY. ONCE he was able to sit up in bed, Aunt Evelyn and I took turns feeding him Cook's warm broth. Mrs. Brumley chittered on and on that she would call in a nurse, but I assured her I would prefer to remain at his side until he left his bed.

My heart felt light, as if the anchor that had been weighing me down had been cut free. I still didn't know what happened. Ferrin continued to put me off, although I pestered him for details again and again. It didn't matter now. Father was going to recover.

Father slept frequently, but during his waking hours, the other guests dropped in to visit with him. It provided a boost to his spirits. Even Mr. and Mrs. Wood came to call. Miss Ansley surprised me with her fortitude at his sickbed and her unwavering attention. But I did not see Colonel Allen, and Charles had not appeared since the day we met in the gardens.

I asked one of the maids about Mr. Brumley's absence when she brought in Father's lunch tray. She told me Mr. Brumley had left Landers Lodge, and she did not know when he would return. Mr. Brumley's departure seemed odd, and I related my thoughts to Ferrin. He shrugged it off and said we were fine enough without him.

Sarah had left London immediately upon receiving my letter and arrived at Landers Lodge before the week's end. It was joyous to have our family united again. Father was so happy I thought he might burst his stitches with the way his chest shook as he chuckled.

"We really ought to let him sleep," I whispered to Sarah.

She touched my shoulder. "You go rest. You have done much good for him, and now it's my turn."

"I'm so glad to see you, Sarah. Mr. Dashel is a lucky man." I loved my sister. We were not always best friends, but she was always a good sister.

I pulled the library door closed softly. My soul felt airy and hopeful and full of joy. I wanted to skip down the hall—until I heard Ferrin's raised voice coming from Charles's book room.

"Have you gone mad, Brumley?" my brother asked before he muttered something else I could not discern.

I approached the door and placed my hand on the knob, but at Charles's next words I froze.

"He is what she wants."

"*Now?* She told you she wanted him *now?*" Ferrin asked with derision.

"No, but I had to do something. You wouldn't let me assist, and it was maddening—walking through every day not knowing when the end would arrive. I would rather put an end to it all at once. If you will finally allow me to speak to your sister, she will know the truth. If I can't be with her, well . . . Wilkins is a good man."

"So you figured you'd break her heart then throw her to the captain with fresh wounds?" That was Mr. Fausett's voice.

"Gads! Do neither of you get it?" Charles asked. "She won't have me. She refused me already, and once I explain what happened, there is no hope. It's too much to ask of her, and I won't do it! Having Captain Wilkins here makes it easier on both of us."

Captain Wilkins was here?

"I may have lost her heart, but I will do all I can not to lose her respect," Charles said.

I charged into the room. "When might I get a say in the matter?"

Ferrin's and Mr. Fausett's eyes shot open wide. Charles grabbed his head and collapsed into his chair, lamenting, "I have such despicable timing."

After giving them all a thorough glare, I turned my attention to Charles. "Mr. Brumley, do you care to explain what is going on, or shall I go find Captain Wilkins and ask him?"

Charles ran his hands through his hair and exhaled loudly. "Ferrin, may I *please* speak with your sister?"

Ferrin looked at me, and I nodded. I could handle whatever Charles had to say.

"Come, Mr. Fausett, I would not recommend remaining in this room." Ferrin walked to the door.

Mr. Fausett raised his eyebrows high and looked between Charles and myself. My shoulders straightened, and I stood at my full height, trying to look unaffected. My heart, which had felt so free only moments ago, thumped wildly in my chest. There was no rhythm to the pounding, just chaotic flutters and jumps. My arms wrapped around my stomach in an attempt to steady the commotion. Mr. Fausett nodded and walked out.

I turned from the door, my gaze moving to Charles. "Mr. Brumley, what do you have to tell me?" It was time to end this. Whatever *this* was.

Charles looked up at me from behind his desk. He wiped his hand over his eyes and slowly stood. With a heavy breath he said, "There are two things actually, but before I begin I have a request."

"Are you really in a position to barter?"

He gave me an exasperated look. "Leah, please."

I sighed melodramatically. "Very well. I'm listening."

"You must hear me out. If this is the last time I will see you, please let me tell you the whole of it before you say good-bye forever." He looked at me like a lost child, and desperation coated his words.

I wanted to tell him to not be so dramatic. There would not be a final good-bye between us. There couldn't be. The thought of never seeing Charles again caused a fierce ache to roil through me and brought my thudding heart back into a steady though extremely painful rhythm. I gave him one curt nod. "Very well. I shall hear you out."

Charles braced his hands on the desk, dropped his head, and pressed his eyes closed. He inhaled deeply and said, "Leah, there is something I have wanted to tell you for some time." He looked up and walked around his desk towards me. He was like a magnificent storm—dangerous and reverent and beautiful. My mouth pinched closed, and my arms wrapped tighter around my middle.

He continued to advance, and my emotions warred within. I wanted him to embrace me, I wanted him to smile, I wanted him to . . . kiss me? And although I wanted all of these beautiful things, the fierce darkness in his eyes told me none of them would happen. And then came relief and hatred and confusion with the knowledge that he would not give me what I wanted. My heartbeat quickened from nerves and desire and an unexplainable sorrow that suddenly enveloped me like a fog. He was so close.

"Leah, do you remember last year when you asked me to stay?"

Another hole opened in my heart at the recollection. There hadn't been a day I didn't remember it.

Charles continued. "You offered me everything, your entire world. And while I knew you were what I wanted," his words caught, and he raised his fingers to my cheek and gently caressed my skin, "what I've always wanted, I refused you."

I closed my eyes and quivered at his touch. He was not fighting fair. His words made no sense. *What he always wanted?* My traitor tears broke free, and Charles dropped his hand. A gasp leapt from my throat, and I quickly covered my mouth. Charles led me to a chair. I hadn't realized how unsteady my legs were until I collapsed into the leather cushion.

Charles knelt down in front of me, holding my hands in one of his; with his other hand, he raised my chin until our eyes met. That sorrowful fog descended on both of us then. "I love you, Leah. I always have. One year ago, I loved you too. But I felt tied down. My father, Mother, you— each of you had expectations for me that I could not fulfill. I didn't want to disappoint you, and I didn't want to despise you for forcing me to choose in that moment.

"It wasn't fair, and you deserved an explanation I could not give. Nor could I ask you to wait when you had given yourself so wholly." He sucked in a deep breath. "When my father died, it made things worse because I didn't have a choice anymore. My future with regard to Riverton Park was decided. The only choice left for me to make was you. I stayed in London, not because I wanted to, but because I realized I wasn't worthy of you. I know I hurt you"—Charles squeezed my fingers a little tighter—"and it has haunted me every day. I was afraid if I came back you would despise me, so it was easier to stay away. That is, until I thought I might lose you to another."

He wrapped both of my hands in his and tenderly kissed my knuckles. It sent traitorous flames through my being. He was telling me why he didn't stay. I should feel anger and resentment: because he fled, because of his silence, because I thought he didn't care. Instead, I didn't want him to ever let me go.

"After walking away I had no hope that you would ever offer your heart again. But when I heard about Captain Wilkins . . . well, I was a jealous fool, and I had to try. I'd thought that perhaps you could forgive me." He shrugged and gave me a small, sad smile. "But you haven't."

"Charles, I—"

"Don't, Leah," he cut me off. Charles stood and only held on to my fingers for a moment more. "It's okay. I was a fool, and you should not have to suffer for my mistakes anymore."

When he released my hands, the warmth fled too. I sat there stripped of everything that had bound us together. A searing ache spread through me, and I could not fathom that he could just walk away—again.

"So you brought Captain Wilkins here?" I forced the words around the pain in my chest. I had to understand. Why did Charles not fight harder now? Why did he not tell me before? Was he fleeing again? Was this really good-bye?

Charles nodded. "I thought I may have been a little brash when I met the poor captain." The grin he offered was obviously strained. "I wanted to make it right so perhaps you could remember me as your friend." There was a profound melancholy in his words.

"Yet again you ramble on and give me no say in the matter," I said on a shaky breath, offering my own forced smile.

Charles walked around the chair, inhaled deeply, and from somewhere behind me, he said, "I don't think I could bear to hear your opinions on this subject—especially not after I tell you the remainder of my confession."

How could there be more? What else did I not know?

And then it struck me as powerful as lightning. The jolt rattled my soul—Father.

I leapt out of my seat and spun to face Charles. "You?" I asked, my voice shaking. "It was you who shot Father?"

"It truly was an accident. I never meant . . ." He stopped and shook his head. Tears glistened in his eyes. "I am so sorry, Leah."

"You're sorry?" I thundered towards him, and he pulled back as he glimpsed the fury in my eyes.

"Ferrin—" he began and took a step back.

"What does Ferrin have to do with this?" I demanded and shoved him hard in the left shoulder.

"He—he asked me not to say anything."

"And you thought that was a good idea?" I advanced another step, forcing Charles to step sideways to avoid colliding with a tall blue vase near the wall.

Charles raised his hands in front of him. "Leah, let me explain."

"Oh, first you're a coward, and now you want to talk?"

He flinched at my accusation, and I pushed him again.

He stepped backwards and took a breath to steady his voice. "You promised to hear me out."

"What do you know about promises, Charles? I trusted you!" I cried out.

"I know."

"You lied to me!" My fists clenched at my side.

"No, Leah, I never lied." He shook his head.

"This is not a game, Charles! You don't even care!" I shouted.

Abruptly he stopped shrinking away and straightened himself to his full height. He held his ground, and my anger boiled inside, watching him stand confident and tall. I wanted to knock him off his pedestal, and I moved to shove him again. Charles grabbed my wrist. I struggled to break his grip and swung at him with my free hand. He grabbed that too. He pulled me towards him; our arms pinned between the two of us. He held me still. Charles's look was intense. I could feel the rise and fall of his chest, the pounding of his heart against my wrists. Frustration and pain simmered with confusion in my gut.

"Leah, please listen," he begged softly. His breath fell like a gentle caress on my face. "I wanted to tell you."

"But you didn't," I whispered with a shaky voice. Then I blinked, and more tears fell.

"Leah—" His voice broke.

"You will address me as Miss Leah." I choked out and yanked my hands free from his grasp. "Better yet, don't address me at all, Mr. Brumley, for I never want to see you again." My whole body shook, but I held my head high as I walked through the door and fled to the sanctuary of my room.

CHAPTER 27
Mr. Charles Brumley

❧

I LOVED LEAH. IT HAD built for years and peaked with a confession that would be my last. I ached—fiercely. The pain gripping my soul was far beyond what I felt when Father died. When he passed, there was nothing to be done. It was God's will, and while I mourned for him, I accepted that it was out of my hands.

However, with Leah I was my own undoing. I callously threw away my first opportunity, and there may have been a second chance if not for the accident. I revisited that moment again and again, wondering what I could have done differently. Should I have only shot once? Did I follow proper safety procedures? It all came back to Admiral. I should have properly stowed my weapon and tended to his needs.

It was not common for Admiral to bark. He had hunted with us the previous days without incident. I should have recognized the dog's altered behavior. Something had been amiss. If only I had taken the time to figure out what it was. If only, if only, if only . . . It was useless to ponder on it any further. Yet I was certain that question would haunt me for the rest of my life.

I should have left Landers Lodge and the guests in the care of my mother, but I would not desert Leah. Not again. Despise me as she may, she could not say I abandoned her now.

Continuously I questioned my justification for bringing Captain Wilkins to Landers Lodge. Somehow in my mind I had convoluted and twisted my logic so it would make sense. Leah was upset. She was hurt, and I had seen Captain Wilkins make her smile. That was all I wanted, for Leah to smile again. The only emotion I seemed to elicit was pain. So Captain Wilkins became part of the plan. If I couldn't bring her joy, maybe he could. And while the strategy resonated with a semblance of truth, it killed me. Picturing Miss Leah with the captain splintered my soul. I did not want to think that he could bring her comfort when I could not. I had always been the one to make her laugh, to collect her smiles. It was not easy to relinquish that right, but I knew I must.

So I had garnered the help of Colonel Allen. The captain was recruited, and I wallowed alone in my misery—wondering where they were, what they were discussing, and if Leah was smiling for Captain Wilkins the way she had once smiled for me.

Fausett was wise enough to give me a wide berth, but after secluding myself to my book room for a third day, he came to see me.

"The doctor said Mr. Hastings may return home in a fortnight," Fausett reported.

"Please pass on my gratitude to the doctor, and let me know when I should make arrangements for the trip."

Fausett looked at my untouched tray of food, and a look of sympathy crossed his face. Wisely, when he looked back at me, his expression was absent of pity. "Very well." He moved to leave.

"Thank you, Devlin," I said, hoping he could hear the sincerity in my voice.

He nodded and reached for the door handle. "May I ask you something?"

I did not respond; in fact, my expression did not change at all.

Whatever Fausett took that to mean, he continued. "Why did you not fight for her?"

I sighed and hung my head, looking at the papers littered across my desk. "It was a battle I could never win."

"How do you know if you never really tried?" He left the thought hanging between us, turned the handle, and walked out.

Never tried? Blasted Fausett! I had come back to win her. I had asked to court her. How did that classify as not trying? I rubbed my hands over my face. I had tried. Just not when I had any chance of success.

CHAPTER 28
Miss Leah Hastings

ↀↈↀ

SURPRISES DID NOT EXCITE ME. So I was very direct with Captain Wilkins and asked him exactly how he came to be at Landers Lodge. He told me Colonel Allen had traveled with Mr. Brumley to his regiment. They explained what had happened to Father and told the captain I was in need of comfort.

At this, Captain Wilkins eyed me apprehensively. He seemed uncertain of the fact that I would call on him to provide such comfort, but he had agreed to come if his leave could be secured. Charles had the foresight to bring the colonel with him and enlisted his help to retain a temporary release of duty for Captain Wilkins. There was nothing left for him to do but return with the men to Landers Lodge.

"I hope it was not presumptuous of me," Captain Wilkins said.

"No." I sighed. "Unexpected is all." It wasn't unpleasant to see the captain again, and had circumstances been different, he would have been most welcome. But with all of the commotion churning through my heart, his presence did not bring the solace I desperately needed.

Father continued to improve. He could now feed himself and had felt well enough to move from his sickbed to a chair near the window. The doctor now only visited every few days and had declared that Father should be able to return home shortly.

It was agreed that Ferrin would ride home early to make preparations and Captain Wilkins would escort Father, Sarah, Aunt Evelyn, and me home shortly after.

Charles had disappeared again, although I knew he remained at Landers Lodge. Wisely, he did not attend dinners and remained holed up in either his bedchamber or his book room. It was unfortunate that his sanctuary was located so near Father's sickroom. Every time I walked past, I was haunted by the memory of Charles's admission. It rekindled my anger each and every day.

⸎

When Gerty came in to open the curtains, she was surprised that I was still in bed.

"Are you feeling quite well, Miss Leah?" she asked.

My body was weak, but I did not feel ill. It had been nearly a week since the dreadful day of Father's accident, and time had taken a toll on my tired eyes and weary heart. "I'm fine, Gerty. Thank you." I sat up. "How is my father this morning?"

Gerty smiled. "He's improving each day, ma'am. Miss Hastings is with him now. I just delivered her breakfast to the library so they could eat together."

Knowing that Sarah was with Father calmed my heart. I was so grateful she had come. I asked Gerty to have a breakfast tray delivered to my room, and she went to make the request.

Half an hour later, Gerty returned. She placed the filled tray on the table near my bed, then I dismissed her. I ate and willed myself to relax. The food settled, and perhaps it was sipping the warm chocolate or the fact that I was treating myself to some tranquility; whatever the reason, I decided to snuggle back down into my blankets.

When I awoke again, it was almost noon. "Lazy girl!" I chastised myself at the same time relishing the rejuvenation sleep had brought. My mind finally felt clear of the haze that had wrapped around me for the last week.

I tugged on the bell pull to call for Gerty and hung my feet over the side of the bed to await her arrival. My muscles ached when I moved, and I stretched my arms high overhead.

Gerty entered. "Good afternoon, Miss Leah."

Her reference to the time brought a smile to my lips. "Yes, it is, Gerty. Did I miss anything this morning?"

My voice felt raw and dry. I reached for the water pitcher on my breakfast tray.

"Nothing to report, ma'am. Miss Hastings asked after you, and I told her you was catching up on sleep is all." Gerty turned to pull a dress from the wardrobe.

When I lifted the pitcher from the tray, a note that had been wedged against the carafe flopped onto its side. I topped my glass with water and picked up the small folded paper square. Across the front in a wobbly scrawl was my name. "Do you know about this?" I turned and held the note towards Gerty.

She shook her head.

"It was on my breakfast tray. Did someone give it to you to deliver this morning?"

"No, miss. I asked Cook to prepare the tray and worked on mending while she did. I only carried it back up to you." Gerty looked frightened, like I was going to reprimand her for a simple note.

"No cause to worry, Gerty." I wanted to set her mind at ease. My voice had been rather abrupt. "I was just curious where it came from."

I set the note on the small desk and quickly slipped into my gown. Bits of anxiety snuck back in while Gerty arranged a simple coif on my head. She curtsied and left.

I moved towards the window and opened the note to read:

Judge not, and ye shall not be judged: condemn not, and ye shall not be condemned: forgive, and ye shall be forgiven. Gospel of Luke, Chapter 6, Verse 37

It was unsigned. I stomped my foot as my temper flared. Who dared send this? It was probably Charles trying to make me feel guilty for another one of his faults.

It was just like his confession. He said he rejected me because of *my* expectations. A stupid excuse! And then he realized he loved me and could not return—again because of me, because I made him feel unworthy. Nonsense! I had pondered his words again and again since that day in his book room because I had not really heard them. My attention was sucked away when he shared the words I had been dying to hear since I was thirteen. He said he loved me—and then he buried the emotion with all sorts of complex, meaningless excuses.

His utterance of love set my heart in a whirl, and then it was brought to an aching halt when he told me Captain Wilkins was here, that I deserved a good man, and he knew I would never have him because he was the one who shot Father.

Within twenty minutes he had professed his love, confessed to shooting Father, and betrothed me to another. He gave me all that I had ever wanted and dismissed me in the same breath, and I hated him for it.

If Charles thought the use of scripture would garner my sympathy, he was wrong. I crumpled the note and tossed it on the ground.

Charles was playing games again. He was employing a new strategy, and he needed to know that I was not willing to be a pawn. Charles would do well to remember that I was the girl who could beat him in a footrace, and I liked the feel of victory.

But I feared that I no longer knew what I was fighting for. Who was my rival? Mrs. Ansley? Charles? Or perhaps myself? I stared out my window at the pond and wept.

Dinner that evening was a quiet affair. The exhaustion I had felt earlier seemed to fall on the entire table. When the men joined us, Ferrin immediately crossed to Catherine, and the two began a quiet discussion. Sarah visited with Rachel, and Mrs. Brumley occupied Aunt Evelyn and Mrs. Ansley. With Charles removed from the party, Mrs. Ansley had been somewhat cordial, at least limiting her torture to only sporadic looks of rebuke. She should know she had won. Mrs. Ansley and Catherine could have Charles and his pitiful excuses. I wished for nothing to do with him.

Mr. Ansley held Captain Wilkins near the door and was quizzing him on his involvement in the Battle of Waterloo. On previous evenings, Captain Wilkins and I had engaged in comfortable conversation about our families, books we had read, or the weather. We would talk until I made my excuses and retired to my room.

Tonight, however, with Captain Wilkins engaged, Mr. Fausett crossed directly to where I sat and addressed me. "How are you faring, Miss Leah?"

"Well enough, I suppose." With an amiable smile, I motioned him to the chair next to me.

He sat down with a straight back and angled himself to look at me. "Very encouraging news about your father," he said.

"Yes, it is. I could not have asked for a better outcome." My smile grew wide with the sincerity of that statement.

Mr. Fausett placated me with a smile, but his eyes turned serious. "Miss Leah, it is not my place, yet I must ask. Have you heard from Brumley"—he cleared his throat—"since that day?"

My leg began to swing, and I rested my hands in my lap to still the involuntary movement. "I—I have not." Did Mr. Fausett refer to the note? He and Charles were old chums. Perhaps he was doing Mr. Brumley's dirty work, following up to make sure I received the rebuke with my breakfast.

"I didn't think so." He sighed and looked down. I studied the profile of his face. He appeared forlorn, despondent.

"Is something the matter?" I suddenly wanted to know why he was so gloomy. It did not appear to be an act, and Mr. Fausett had always radiated such a happy countenance.

He quickly lifted his expression and gave me a forced smile. He took a breath and appeared as if he were about to speak; however, he stopped short of actually saying anything.

"Mr. Fausett?" I pressed.

"'Tis nothing. I just hope in the end everything will be put to rights."

Rachel approached. "Pardon me, Miss Leah." Then turning to Mr. Fausett, she smiled sweetly. "My brother is asking for you, Mr. Fausett."

"Yes, of course." And with that, he excused himself.

Watching him leave, I wondered again if the two were cohorts. Mr. Fausett had appeared truly burdened, and I contemplated what weight he carried.

Mrs. Ansely suddenly stood before me. "I hope you are not conspiring against my admonishment, Miss Leah," she hissed.

"Excuse me?" I asked. It was unfortunate that her kindness had only been a charade.

Mrs. Ansley waddled nearer. She preened her skirt while pinching her mouth tight. With excessive show she sat beside me on the sofa. I shifted slightly away and held my chin high.

"Miss Leah," she looked down her nose and feigned a friendly smile, "these games are becoming old." Mrs. Ansley straightened a fold in her dress. "Perhaps you think my previous warning idle?"

"You would be incorrect, Mrs. Ansley, for I believe you very capable of extortion."

"Extortion?" She waved a hand towards me and laughed lightly. "Silly girl." Mrs. Ansley's dramatics were a better fit for the theater than my patience.

"What exactly would you call your threat?"

She dropped her frivolous laugh and stared at me with her beady little eyes. "Just a simple warning."

I matched her quiet tone. "Father's still unable to leave his sickroom, and you have the audacity to threaten me? You are not the woman I thought you to be, Mrs. Ansley. My sympathies to your poor daughter."

"Catherine does not need your sympathy, for she will soon be Mr. Brumley's bride. I simply wanted to remind you to stay out of the way."

"As you know, Captain Wilkins is here on my account because Mr. Brumley fetched him. Mr. Brumley has been noticeably absent these past few days, and I assure you, I have no desire to see him. You are welcome to Mr. Brumley; in fact, you deserve each other." I let out a single laugh. "The one I pity in the match is your kind daughter. She deserves better than the both of you."

Mrs. Ansley sputtered in response.

"Good night, Mrs. Ansley." I stood and walked away not looking back at her crooked neck. I've always despised geese.

The next morning, Ferrin assisted Father as he walked small circles in the library. Father kept his arm in a sling, but otherwise he was improving quite well. Captain Wilkins was riding with Mr. Fausett, and I decided to head outdoors.

While walking past the drawing room, I heard Rachel's theatrical whine. "Mother, Charles promised a ball!"

I peeked through the door and saw Rachel pouting with her arms flung across her chest. It was a reminder of the stories Charles had shared about her dramatics and brought a smile to my lips.

"Things have changed, Rachel," Mrs. Brumley gently replied. "I cannot get Charles to show his face at dinner, nor speak to me. It's irrational to believe he will host a ball."

"Miss Leah could get him to do it," Rachel said so matter-of-factly it startled me.

"Hush, girl!" Mrs. Brumley warned and waved a hand at her daughter.

"Do you have time to cancel the event?" Sarah asked. She sat against the far window, and I had not realized she was in the room.

Aunt Evelyn clucked her disparagement as she stitched away. "Dear Mr. Clem always said, 'Once you set a rock in motion, you no longer get to control the damage.'" Her opinion seemed to be the general sentiment.

"We can inform all of our closest neighbors, of course, but I doubt we can reach the others in time." Mrs. Brumley sounded genuinely concerned. It was no small undertaking to cancel a ball once the invitations had been sent. As Aunt Evelyn had pointed out, there was no undoing the thing.

"Oh, for heaven's sake. Hold the ball." I stomped into the room, and Rachel's face lit with a grin. Aunt Evelyn smirked as well, but surprisingly she held her tongue. Only the prick of her needle and the pulling of the thread could be heard.

Sarah cornered me with a look of challenge. "What about Mr. Brumley? He has shown no inclination to host such an event."

"He knows what it means to be a gentleman." The words came naturally, and I felt a stab of something inside as I made the statement. I pondered the truth of my words. *Did* Mr. Brumley know what it meant to be a gentleman? The tightness released quickly with the realization that, yes, he did. For all the many reasons I despised Charles, none of them had to do with his sense of propriety or decorum. Even his bringing Captain Wilkins to Landers Lodge, in his eyes, had been a gentlemanly endeavor.

"He won't speak with Mother," Rachel whined.

Certainly Rachel was simply being dramatic again. I looked at Mrs. Brumley to refute the claim.

"It's true," Mrs. Brumley confirmed. "Mr. Fausett is the only one Charles will see." Mrs. Brumley turned away, obviously bothered by her son's exclusion. Perhaps this was the reason Mr. Fausett had asked about my interaction with Mr. Brumley.

"Enlist Mr. Fausett's help, then. He is a good man and certainly understands the importance of having a proper host when the guests arrive." I gave a definitive nod, certain that the problem would now be resolved. But just to solidify the situation, I added, "And if Mr. Brumley is not convinced to see it through, tell him Captain Wilkins might stand in his place." I watched Sarah's eyes widen with reproach, and Mrs. Brumley's mouth hung open until she covered it with her hand. Rachel kept grinning, and Aunt Evelyn laughed out loud.

I exited the drawing room with a superior sense of satisfaction. It was wrong to pit the two men against each other, but Captain Wilkins was here because Mr. Brumley had invited him. Mr. Brumley had insisted that the captain was a good man. So really it was all Charles's doing.

Let's see who could place blame now.

CHAPTER 29
Mr. Charles Brumley

❧

"SHE WANTS ME TO WHAT?" I yelled incredulously.

"It's too late to notify everyone, Brumley," Fausett said. "You know there's nothing more to be done. You must host the ball." He was far too casual about that assertion.

I paced in front of the fireplace then paused and put my hands on my hips. "What if I refuse? What then?"

A small smile crept across Fausett's face. "Miss Leah suggested that if you refuse, Captain Wilkins could act as host."

Anger welled within me like a rising tide. "Find this funny, do you?" I loathed Fausett's gloating expression.

He gave an unrepentant shrug. "Miss Leah suggested that since you had invited him and claimed he was such a good man, should you find yourself indisposed, you would be willing to acquiesce to Captain Wilkins." Fausett walked towards the door.

I grabbed the letter salver that sat on my desk and chucked it at him. He ducked and laughed as he let himself out.

There was nothing even slightly amusing about it! Mother had sent the invitations for the ball, and during the commotion of Mr. Hastings's injury and recovery, no one had thought to cancel the blasted thing. Now, in five days' time, my home would be invaded with neighbors and vague acquaintances eager for a free meal and a dance. I could not stomach the thought.

Listening near my door, I verified no one was near and then slipped outside to the stables.

Faster and faster I pushed Mouse. It was harsh to make him run so hard in the brisk air, but I needed to feel the slap of the wind in my face. My confinement had lasted far too long.

On the back of the magnificent animal, the chill wrapped around me, and I could fixate on the thrill of the moment. I didn't want it to end. I didn't want to go back to feeling isolated and defeated, broken and bruised. The freedom I had desired for so long came at too dear a cost.

With a quick tug on the reins, Mouse slowed to a menial trot. I gave his neck a hearty rub. The intoxication subsided, and instantly my problems returned. What was I to do?

It seemed Mother and Leah had left me with little choice. I had to host a ball.

CHAPTER 30
Miss Leah Hastings

CHARLES HAD AGREED. RELUCTANTLY, ACCORDING to Mr. Fausett, but he agreed, nonetheless.

The crisp air cleared my head and forced me to pull my coat tighter around me. I huffed into my gloved hands, wondering why I tortured myself in the cold weather. As I neared the far end of the gardens, my eyes were drawn from the path by the sounds of a rider approaching from the direction of the pond.

Captain Wilkins had been taking regular rides with Mr. Fausett. Today they had ridden to town to place some orders for Mrs. Brumley's preparations. I did not expect them back so soon.

I shielded my eyes from the sun and saw Charles astride his brown gelding. He stopped, and the air ceased to be cold.

We stood like that, staring at one another, too far to speak yet close enough to feel the taut emotion between us. The air buzzed with electric anticipation, waiting for something to snap. It finally did. Charles kicked Mouse forward and rode on.

My hands had clenched into fists, and my fingers began to slowly relax. I stared at where Charles had stood until another memory flashed before my eyes—the image of Ferrin carrying Father, wounded and bleeding, to the house. Burning anger snuffed out all the warmth I had felt. I turned on my heel and headed inside.

After checking on Father and finding him asleep, I went to my room to compose myself. I tossed my bonnet on the bed and crossed to the window. A piece of paper on my writing desk caught my eye, and I discovered a second note on the table in the same wobbly scrawl.

> *And be ye kind one to another, tenderhearted, forgiving one*
> *another, even as God for Christ's sake hath forgiven you.*
> *Ephesians, Chapter 4, Verse 32*

The man had no shame! How did he deliver the missive so quickly? Perhaps Fausett was not his coconspirator since he was in town, or perhaps Charles had enlisted the help of a servant.

I called for Gerty, but after extensive questioning, she could not unravel any more of the mystery as to how the note reached my chambers.

My frustration compounded to anger, and it took an entire hour of pacing for my emotions to unwind. When I left my room, I found Sarah sitting with Father in the library, writing to our Aunt Barnes.

"What do you make of this?" I dropped the note on the paper in front of her.

"Leah! The ink is not yet dry!" She hastily removed my note from hers and skimmed the contents. "Where did this come from?"

"It was left on the writing desk in my room," I explained.

Father sat quietly in his chair, staring out the window.

"Who is it from?" Sarah asked.

"Mr. Brumley, of course!"

"Are you quite certain?"

"Well, yes! Who else would send such a poignant missive?"

Sarah read the verse aloud. "'And be ye kind one to another, tender-hearted, forgiving one another, even as God for Christ's sake hath forgiven you.' What do you make of it, Father?" she asked.

"You can't argue with the good book," he said simply, never taking his eyes off the windowpane.

I huffed and opened my mouth to object to my father's assessment, but Sarah spoke first. "Leah." Sarah's matronly voice irked me. "What are you holding against Mr. Brumley?"

I scoffed. "Father's accident, of course!"

"So you confess it was an accident?"

I shot her an icy look, which she returned with a reproving glare of her own. The truth was I knew it was an accident, though every other time I had referred to it as Father's incident or Father's injury.

"What bothers you most—the fact that it was Charles's weapon? Would you unleash this same contempt on a servant or Ferrin had they been the guilty party?" Sarah watched me as I pondered her question.

I blurted out, "I don't know! But had it been a servant, I would have known immediately! I could have come to terms with the truth instead of being blissfully ignorant for days on end."

"Ferrin knew, yet you do not hold him in contempt."

"Ferrin was doing what he thought was best. His focus was on Father, not self-preservation."

"So you think Mr. Brumley avoided telling you because he was worried for himself?" Why did Sarah make it sound so black and white?

"I don't know why Mr. Brumley held his tongue. If I hadn't overheard their shouts, he may still be keeping the truth concealed."

"That is neither true nor fair, Leah. Mr. Brumley was respecting Ferrin's wishes. Ferrin confirmed as much. Perhaps you could ask our brother his reasons. Then some of your wrath could spread to him as well." She was so calm, sitting with one hand in her lap, the other resting on the table. It riled me more.

"Mr. Brumley is his own man. He should have told me rather than recruit Captain Wilkins to clean up his mess," I said.

"Are you sure this is not about something more?" Sarah asked.

"Of course not!" It was a lie because every time I thought back on that evening I did not remember Charles's confession about the shooting. I remembered him declaring his love then ripping out my heart and handing it over to Captain Wilkins. The problem with his plan was that my wounds continued to fester and there was nothing the good captain could do to heal them.

CHAPTER 31
Mr. Charles Brumley

❧ ⚜ ❧

MOTHER WAS GRANTED FREE REIGN of the ball, and Fausett was tasked with informing me of the time to appear. He found the whole situation amusing and took every opportunity to fluster me.

Saturday finally arrived, and I ventured again to the stables to clear my mind. Seeing Leah earlier in the week had been a mixture of joy and sadness. She did not flee upon seeing me, nor did she move to acknowledge me.

Yet neither did I.

I waited, watching to see which direction I should go. The moment held still, frozen and lingering between us. It was not rejection, but neither was it forgiveness. As time stilled, sorrow pressed my heart until it was more than I could endure. Without hope, I had returned to the stables.

This morning, as I led my horse out of the gate, Fausett appeared.

"Morning, Brumley. Mind if I join you?" he asked.

I eyed him cautiously. A teasing grin threatened to spill across his mouth, but he composed himself and waited patiently while I answered. "Very well. If you can refrain from riling me further with any mention of this cursed ball."

"That I can do. Give me a moment." He disappeared into the stables.

Although Fausett had agreed not to rile me, I refused to even give him the opportunity. I rode hard, galloping over the frozen ground. My breath evaporated in a white cloud before my eyes. I was not looking forward to tonight. I had not entertained much since my father's funeral, and then only dinners, which Mother concocted. Never had I been the host of a ball.

Yet it was not the duties of decorum that were agitating me. I could greet the guests and put on a stoic face, but it would rip me apart to watch Leah dance happily in Captain Wilkins's arms. I had determined that there was no reason for me to stay and torment myself. I could stand and welcome the arrivals, lead out the first dance with Rachel, then retire.

With a tug on the reins, Mouse slowed, and the chill of exhilaration fell away as the warmth from my body overtook it.

Fausett pulled his horse alongside me. "Do you run all your horses this hard?"

I ignored him and looked straight ahead.

"It's surprising you still have a warm body in your stables," he said.

"The breeder appreciates the business," I said dryly.

Fausett chuckled.

We rode to the edge of the trees to cool the horses off, then turned back towards the paddock.

"Are you ready for tonight?" Fausett asked.

"I thought you agreed not to talk about the ball." I gave him a sharp look.

He held my gaze for a moment then looked forward across the meadow. "I wasn't referring to the ball."

I sighed. "Am I that transparent?"

He smirked, giving me my answer.

"What am I to do?" I asked.

"There was a reason you succeeded at Cambridge, Brumley. It's the same reason we ended up friends." My eyebrows rose in question. "Remember when you prepared your discourse on proving Newton's Principia? Professor Atkins said it lacked conviction. You returned the next day and delivered a two-hour lecture expounding the veracity of the laws of motion and universal gravitation, which surpassed every attempt he had made to explain the theorem."

The memory of that triumph brought a smile to my lips. It had been a heady feeling, to be sure.

"I've never seen you back down from a challenge. Is this any different?" Fausett asked.

"Professor Atkins tried to obstruct my goal. I did what I needed to overcome that obstacle. Matters of the mind I can wrestle and win. Matters of the heart are an entirely different matter."

"Actually, my friend, they are not that different. Go, man! Go fight for her!" Fausett kicked his horse forward and disappeared into the stables.

CHAPTER 32
Miss Leah Hastings

❦

ASSISTING WITH THE PREPARATIONS FOR the ball had been a welcome distraction. Sarah and I rotated sitting with Father and aiding Mrs. Brumley. Mrs. June ran the household with an experienced hand, and within a matter of days, Landers Lodge had transformed into a whimsical refuge.

In Mrs. Brumley's attempt to satisfy Rachel's expectations, the décor was exquisite. Green garlands festooned every doorway, and colorful gourds were situated in the boughs spread along the tables. Dozens of flowers had been secured from nearby hothouses and were placed throughout Landers Lodge in intricate arrangements. Flickering candles completed the ambiance, providing a warm and welcome retreat from the cool autumn air.

I purposely delayed joining the others until I was certain the guests had begun to arrive. Charles had agreed to host and would therefore be occupied, making it easy to avoid him.

Upon returning to my room to prepare for the festivities, I received a third, unsigned letter, written in the same hand. It simply read:

> *We forgive to the extent that we love.*
> *Francois de La Rochefoucauld*

I could not decide if Charles's not-so-subtle quotes amused me or infuriated me. His preaching most definitely did not amuse me, but his approach I found quite humorous. Until the past year, we had always had such an easy way with words, so I took it to heart that he was so frightened he resorted to sending unsigned missives. He was my solitary suspect and the only soul brave enough to be so bold.

I dressed in my muslin gown with short capped sleeves and trim the color of butter. I instructed Gerty to make my hair simple but elegant. We agreed on a tasteful coiffure that emphasized my abundance of curls, and Gerty secured a matching cream ribbon with expertly hidden pins.

I descended the staircase quickly, not wishing to draw attention to myself. Near the bottom of the stairs, I adjusted my gloves and glanced towards the throng in the entryway. One person stood out. He always stood out.

Charles stood, greeting the guests, his posture refined and authoritative. His hair was slightly mussed, which made him appear naturally confident. Charles stood regal in his formal black coat and crisp white cravat, and while I knew better than to stare, it could not be helped.

I had missed him, and I did not realize how much until that moment. We were scheduled to leave Landers Lodge in two days, and the uncertainty of when I might see him again rooted me to the spot. I wanted to absorb all of Charles's presence, to store it away in an effort to somehow retain a part of what once was.

The contents of the most recent note floated through my mind: *We forgive to the extent that we love.* Did I love Charles? Could I forgive him? For the first time, I wondered if the answer to both questions could be yes. I grasped the stair rail to secure myself from the sudden dizziness that swept from my mind down through my heart.

Then Charles turned and saw me. His eyes filled with concern as he observed my unsteady state. He ignored the elderly woman in front of him, and when she followed his attention, my face warmed and my knees weakened.

I contemplated sitting on the step behind me when a firm hand took my elbow. "Miss Leah, are you quite all right?" Captain Wilkins asked. He stood on the ground level and assisted me down the final step. His steady strength allowed me to regain my bearings.

"Thank you," I whispered. When I turned to look back towards the entrance, I could no longer see Charles.

"What impeccable timing you have, Captain," Mrs. Ansley said as she sauntered near us.

"Good evening, Mrs. Ansley." Captain Wilkins tilted his head, his hold on me secure and unwavering.

Mrs. Ansley remained in our way, penetrating my resolve with her cold, beady eyes. "Miss Leah, you should count yourself fortunate. Not all gentlemen are as attentive to the needs of those in their care."

I stiffened at her veiled reference to her accusations of my father.

"If you will please excuse us," Captain Wilkins said firmly. Mrs. Ansley stepped aside with a satisfied sneer. Captain Wilkins pulled my hand through his arm and led me towards the ballroom. "Miss Leah, you look beautiful tonight."

My eyes perused his figure, and after several more breaths, my nerves began to steady. Captain Wilkins looked handsome as well, but my heart did not behave as it had when I saw Charles. I felt relaxed when I looked at Captain Wilkins's clear blue eyes smiling back at me. I was not moved or weakened or brought to recollect quotations about love. I could not decide which emotion I preferred.

"Thank you for your assistance, Captain Wilkins. The sheer number of guests must have been too pressing for me. I was not expecting such a deluge this evening."

"It's my pleasure." Turning towards me, he slid my arm out of his and held my fingers. "If you are feeling well enough and are not otherwise engaged, may I request your hand for the first dance?"

"I would be honored." It wasn't a lie. Captain Wilkins was a gentleman in every respect. It was an honor to have his regard.

Charles led Rachel out for the first dance, and when Captain Wilkins and I moved to the floor, it took all of my willpower not to look at my old friend. Instead, I stared at the lapels of Captain Wilkins's jacket.

I successfully avoided Charles throughout the course of the dance; however, once the music ended, I found myself scanning the room in search of him, wanting to discover where he had gone.

Mrs. Ansley worked quickly. She dragged Catherine across the floor and practically threw the poor girl into Charles's arms. They moved towards the floor as Ferrin appeared and asked me to dance. Captain Wilkins thanked me for my hand, bowed to my brother, and left us.

We took our position in the line of couples, but I did not want to be there. "Could we perhaps talk instead of dance?" I asked Ferrin.

He looked at me thoughtfully. "Shall we go see to Father?"

"An excellent suggestion."

Father was comfortably settled in his bed, enjoying a book on philosophy. The pallor had finally left his face. His cheeks had resumed their jovial roundness, and he chastised us for doting on him rather than joining the festivities. I reminded him that he would always be our priority.

"Oh, posh," Father exclaimed when I brought him an extra blanket. "Go dance," he commanded and quickly shooed us away.

As Ferrin escorted me back towards the ballroom, I touched his arm. He stopped and turned towards me.

"Why did you not tell me about Mr. Brumley's part in Father's—" I caught my breath. I had been about to say *injury*; instead, I finished, "Accident?"

"It was not my place to tell you," Ferrin answered.

"No, it was not. However, you refused to let Mr. Brumley disclose the truth. Why?" It suddenly became imperative for me to know.

"Leah, now is not the time for this. Let's get back to the ball." Ferrin turned to continue down the hall, but I stood rooted in place, gripping his arm.

"No, Ferrin. Then was not a good time. Now is not a good time. When *will* be a good time to discuss this?" My voice rose. "What are you not telling me?"

"I have no secrets, Leah," Ferrin said calmly.

"Mr. Brumley does, then?" I asked.

"Did he confess his feelings for you?"

My breath caught at Ferrin's boldness. "Yes," I whispered and curled my lips to keep them from quivering.

"Then he has no secrets either."

Confusion filled my face, begging him to explain.

Ferrin sighed then said, "Leah, if Brumley has told you he loves you, then everything has been revealed. The only secrets left are yours."

"What do you mean?" I dug my fingers deeper, clenching his forearm.

His eyes swept my face, questioning my resolve. When he saw my determination, he answered with a new intensity. "Do you really want to know why I didn't tell you? Do you want to know why I asked Brumley to stay silent?" He stepped close, breathing down his frustration on me.

"Yes," I cried.

"Because I didn't want to break your heart," Ferrin said with fervor. I startled and pulled back. Ferrin's eyes softened, and he continued. "You have the biggest secret of all. You love him as he loves you. He finally admitted it, but you are holding your tongue. You hold a grudge better than anyone I know. I knew you wouldn't forgive him even though you love him." I dropped my hand from his arm and stared at the marble floor. "I was only trying to postpone the heartache as long as possible." Ferrin reached for my fingers. He gave my gloved hand a gentle squeeze. "I would have concealed the truth forever if I thought I could. But Brumley was determined to not keep it a secret. He insisted that you be told the truth. I'm sorry if I caused you more pain."

I raised my eyes to his. He pressed my hand one more time and, after a deep breath, released me. "I'll see you inside," he said and walked away.

The dizziness I felt before was nothing compared to the disorientation I felt now. I stumbled down the hall to Charles's book room. The door was unlocked, and I let myself inside.

The fire burned bright, and I fell into one of the leather armchairs. It was the same one Charles had directed me to when he made his confessions.

The room reflected him perfectly. The rich tones of the rock fireplace and the strong wooden desk that dominated the room reminded me of the constant he had always been in my life. Until recent years, it was a constant that was comfortable, like the worn solid leather on the chairs. Now it was a constant fraught with uncertainty. I was constantly unsure, constantly wondering what would come next from him. It was an unpredictability that rattled the core of our friendship. Maybe I couldn't even call it a friendship anymore.

Ferrin's words stung like a slap in the face. If it was my secret, what gave Ferrin the right to expose it? I had not denied my feelings for Charles a year ago. My declaration of love had gotten me nowhere. Charles had run, and our relationship had become strained and tainted.

After meeting Captain Wilkins, I thought I had put Charles from my mind. But my realization a month ago on the road—and again this evening on the stairs—illuminated the truth as clearly as the light flickering across the room. I had pushed Mr. Brumley from my mind, yet he still held a place in my heart. It was a place that refused to be filled by Captain Wilkins, Mrs. Ansley, or anger over my father being shot. It would always belong exclusively to Charles, and he was the only one that could fill the vast emptiness.

A tear rolled down my cheek. *We forgive to the extent that we love.* Ferrin was right: I loved Charles. But was it enough to forgive him?

CHAPTER 33
Mr. Charles Brumley

❧

MOTHER HAD INVITED FAR TOO many people. Finally, the introductions were complete, as was my mandatory dance with Rachel. Leah danced with Captain Wilkins, but it hadn't flustered me as I feared it would.

She refused to look at me, yet I watched her through every turn. Her eyes were not on me, but neither were they on Captain Wilkins. She avoided his gaze as acutely as she avoided mine.

Once the dance finished, I returned Rachel to my mother and asked Fausett to keep an eye on the vultures circling my little sister. I glanced around the room, searching for Leah. I did not see her; however, I did see Captain Wilkins approach Miss Hastings. Knowing he was not exclusively dancing with Leah provided some relief. I turned to retreat and found myself face-to-face with Mrs. Ansley.

"Oh, Mr. Brumley!" she cawed. "You would not have Catherine sit out this dance when you are without a partner?" Miss Ansley stumbled as her mother pushed her towards me.

I had every intention of telling Mrs. Ansley what I thought of her matchmaking tactics, but one look at Miss Ansley and I could not. The poor girl was mortified. "Would you do me the honor, Miss Ansley?" I extended my hand.

Once we were out of earshot of her mother, Miss Ansley said, "I do apologize, Mr. Brumley. You are not obligated to dance with me."

"Would you rather remain at your mother's side?" I asked.

She blushed and looked down at the floor. "Well, no. She admires you, Mr. Brumley, as do I, but perhaps one day I will have the courage to tell her that while I respect her opinion, I do not always agree with it."

The musicians began the lively dance, and before the steps began, I saw Miss Ansley peer down the line to where Ferrin led Leah away from the floor.

"Yes. Perhaps one day, Miss Ansley," I agreed with a smile, and we began the dance.

When the dance concluded, I escorted Miss Ansley to my mother and gave my excuses. Mother sent me a disapproving glare, but I turned away, seeking the security of my book room.

When I stepped through the door, Leah jumped up from a chair and spun to face me.

"Mr. Brumley," she said in surprise.

The fire flickered behind Leah, masking her eyes in shadows. I wanted to know what brought her here and, more importantly, what kept her from fleeing now that we stood in the same room.

Her gaze followed me as I walked around to the fireplace. My new angle provided a different view; flames now danced in her speckled eyes, and I didn't want to move for fear of breaking the moment. A different sort of feeling settled between us. Gone was the anger I'd seen before, replaced by something I could not quite determine.

We stood passive and peaceful for a long minute.

"Forgive me, Mr. Brumley." Her voice was soft and almost pleading.

She made to leave, and I called her name. She glanced back and offered a genuine smile before gently sliding out the door.

I remained standing, staring at the place where Leah disappeared. Why had she been here? She left, but she had not fled. Nor was she angry or vengeful. What had happened?

Like a punch in the gut, I wondered if her tolerance of me was due to a change of circumstance. I no longer yearned for the sanctuary of my room. The confines of its walls were punishing. I could only wonder what was taking place down the hall. If feelings of love or, heaven forbid, proposals of marriage, were being discussed. I could not bear to think on it a second more and immediately returned to the strains of music floating from the ballroom.

Leah danced with Fausett. I breathed a sigh of relief, even if it was only temporary. They remained on the floor for two sets, and then Fausett escorted Leah to her sister. The musicians retook their instruments, and the waltz began. Captain Wilkins moved towards Leah, but I could intercept her first. It was to be a race then. I took the first step, wondering what kind of a fool's errand I had set upon. Another step forward, and I felt a hand on my arm.

"Let them be, Brumley," Fausett said.

I looked back at Leah; she smiled as Captain Wilkins bowed and led her to a position on the floor. Drat!

"Unhand me!" I shook off Fausett's grip and turned on him. "First you tell me to fight, then you tell me to let her be." I barely kept my voice tempered.

"Patience, Brumley," Fausett warned and nodded towards the floor. "I think perhaps your appearance tonight was enough."

"I have no idea to what you are referring," I said through clenched teeth, but Fausett was no longer looking at me. Instead, he watched Leah and Captain Wilkins turn around the floor.

Leah smiled at the captain, and it made me sick to my stomach. Why did I ever think to bring him here? Fausett's amused grin angered me. "Find this funny, do you?" I asked. "I shall never understand your warped sense of humor."

It was a fitting punishment, watching them smile at each other, swaying in rhythm with the music. My heart ached with a fierce jealousy.

Fausett turned to me. "I love a happy ending," he said with decisive finality.

Leah and the captain disappeared into the crowd, and I glared at Fausett, wanting to wipe that smug grin off with a well-placed facer. My hands clenched, and I took a deep breath.

Rachel stepped up. "Oh, Charles, I knew you had not abandoned me!" She grabbed my hand, not realizing the fist I held was destined for Fausett's jaw. "Mother said you left, but I told her you were a better brother than that and surely you would return for a second dance."

I had not looked at Rachel. My eyes were trained on Fausett and his cocky smirk. He raised his brows and nodded towards my sister. Rachel tugged on my arm, and I reluctantly turned in her direction. "Please, Charles, there are only a few dances left." She batted her eyelashes with perfection and found my weakness.

"I am not in a mood to dance, Rachel," I warned her.

"Pleeease, Charles?" she begged with her hands clasped below her chin.

"You do know it's not proper for a lady to be begging partners. You should wait for the gentleman to ask you," I said and felt my reserve slipping.

"They've all been scared away by Mr. Fausett. You asked him to keep an eye on me, and I'm afraid he has effectively terrified anyone who would ask me to dance."

I cast a look at Fausett, who shrugged and offered an unrepentant grin. Perhaps I would have to apologize later for wanting to throttle him—much later. "Very well, Rachel." I took her hand and bowed low. "Would you care to dance?"

She giggled and with a curtsy said, "I would be delighted."

I rolled my eyes with derision then led Rachel to the floor.

The motions were mindless, and I engaged the time scanning the room for a head of dark curly hair. I could locate neither Leah nor Captain Wilkins, and my patience was wearing thin, but the look of contentment on Rachel's face kept my feet moving in time to the music. I had vowed to be a better brother. I would not fail there as well.

When the song ended, I looked over the top of Rachel's head and saw Captain Wilkins conversing with Mr. Ansley. Leah was not with him.

The musicians prepared for another number, and I longed for just one dance with her. It would ruin me because one would never be enough, not when I wanted to claim them all. But for the numerous dances we had attended together—private balls, the Assembly Hall, even impromptu dances in our parlor—we had always danced at least one dance. It would be tragic to break that tradition tonight.

I circled the floor, ignoring those who wished to speak to me. When I passed near, Mrs. Ansley had the audacity to grab for my arm. I shook her off and continued to look and search in vain. Leah was not to be found. Captain Wilkins had taken the floor with Rachel. I stopped abruptly, ready to deny him her hand, then just as quickly acknowledged that Rachel was in no danger from the captain. He was my guest, and Fausett was still very aware of his commitment to act as sentry to my sister.

While I was somewhat perturbed that the handsome captain was dancing with Rachel, I was abundantly relieved that Leah was not his partner. Where could she be? I returned to Fausett's side, hawkishly watching my sister. "Have you seen Miss Leah?" I asked.

"Not since she left with Captain Wilkins," Fausett said.

I motioned impatiently at the dance floor. "Yes, but as you are aware, he has returned, and she has not."

"Hmm." Fausett contemplated. "Perhaps they concluded their business and Miss Leah was not in a mood to return to the dance."

He looked at me with a completely straight face. He could rile me so. I found it much more entertaining when he turned his wit on someone else. I growled at him and could hear his laughter as I left the room.

It was too cold to be outside, so I assumed Leah had gone to bed. Questions swirled through my mind. Conversation, music, and laughter poured into the hall and mixed into a giant wave of chaos and confusion.

I pulled a candle off the sconce outside my book room and stepped inside. Again Leah sat in one of the leather chairs.

This time she did not jump when I entered; she stood slowly and looked at me. In the quiet of the room, I could hear her catch her breath. It was the only movement between us. I dared not breathe for fear of what would come next.

I stood with a candle in one hand; the other remained on the doorknob. The noise from the ballroom disappeared—all except the music.

Win her! Fausett's words rang clear. I had to try.

"I was just contemplating . . ." I began. I walked to the desk and set the candle down. "I would hate to break our streak."

Leah tilted her head but did not respond. The light danced across her face, the shadows drawing me to the mystery and the light magnifying her beauty.

I collected my wits. "There has not been a time when we have attended a gathering together and not shared at least one dance." My heartbeat felt like a caged dove, flapping and beating and fighting for freedom. I extended my hand. "Shall we dance, Miss Leah?"

Leah's eyebrows righted themselves, and without a word she walked over and put her hand in mine. With that acceptance the wings on my heart spread wide. I pulled her towards me and placed my hand upon her waist. In the solitude of that small space, we danced the final refrains of the song.

When the music ended, I did not let her go. I kept one arm around her and tangled her fingers in mine. She made no move to withdraw, and we stood spellbound, tied to one another with an intensity unlike anything I had ever felt. We stood close, but I longed to draw her nearer. Yet I feared if I moved, the moment would shatter, and my heart could not survive another fatal blow.

So we stood like statues, staring at one another, breathing and feeling so alive and so volatile at the same time. Without realizing, I raised Leah's hand to my lips and tenderly placed a kiss on each of her knuckles. She closed her eyes as my lips brushed her skin again, and I could not resist anymore. I tightened my hold on her waist and pulled her closer. I leaned forward to place a final kiss on her lips. A mere breath separated us when her eyes flew open and she stepped away. My hand fell from her side, but she did not release my fingers.

The fervent intensity instantly retreated. The spark of emotion was severed except where she held my hand in hers. She tightened her hold on my fingers and said, "We forgive to the extent that we love."

"What?" I asked.

"I forgive you, Charles," Leah said. The lines of her face were soft and filled with peace. She quickly continued. "For Father's accident. I realize it was just that—an accident." She placed her free hand on my arm. "I'm sorry it took me so long to realize."

"I—" I started, trying to compose myself enough to think rationally.

"Thank you for the dance," she said. And then she slipped out the door and was gone.

CHAPTER 34

Miss Leah Hastings

ဢ‌ଏ

THE FOLLOWING DAY WAS FILLED with preparations for our departure. I had not told anyone about my epiphany, my sudden forgiveness of Charles, that I had to forgive him because my heart would not have it any other way. The truth of that knowledge lifted a heavy burden from my heart.

During our travel, the rain would not relent. The carriage was well sprung, but the journey thus far had been tolerable at best. Sarah had praised Mrs. June's forethought to send extra blankets in the carriage. Father, Aunt Evelyn, Sarah, and I huddled together, swaddled in mounds of quilts. Captain Wilkins was an honor to his profession. He remained astride his horse through the nonstop downpour. He did not have my heart, but my respect for him grew immensely.

The carriage jostled, and Father winced in pain. "We're approaching an inn. Do you wish to stop and rest?" I asked him.

"No, my dear," Father answered. "I would rather push through and reach Astoria as soon as possible."

We arrived home three hours later. Ferrin had returned the day prior to prepare for Father's needs. He met the carriage and, with the assistance of Jensen and Captain Wilkins, helped Sarah and me situate Father in his room. Aunt Evelyn retired immediately.

A warm, blazing fire burned in the fireplace of my chamber. Gerty was an angel. It was a strange sensation to be home again. To be in my familiar room, where nothing had changed and to contemplate that, outside of these walls, a metamorphosis had occurred.

When I was eight years old, my mother had purchased a new dress for me for Christmas. It was white satin with a large red bow and flowing skirt. When I twirled, the satin soundlessly spun around and around. I felt like a princess. On Christmas Eve I had worn the dress to dinner, and afterward we opened gifts. My cousin Nora was given a new set of paints. She opened the new tubes and tested each color on a piece of parchment. In her excitement that the blue truly was royal in color, she spun around with her paintbrush in hand and decorated my beautiful white dress with a royal-blue stripe.

She was, of course, mortified and apologized profusely. I spouted words that were much too cruel, ran to my room, and did not speak to her for the rest of the holiday. Mother tried to coax me out of my silence, but I refused to even look at Nora. That was the last holiday my cousin spent with us.

For twelve years, when I thought of my cousin, I remembered my ruined dress. Why was it only now that I remembered the silly games she and I would play or the tea parties we would have with our dolls or the walks we took to pick wildflowers hand in hand?

Ferrin was right. I did hold a grudge long and hard and too close to my heart to forgive. Charles's confession, his sorrowful eyes, and the acknowledgment of my own heart showed me that I was missing something I never knew was lost.

I sat down at my desk right then and composed a letter to my cousin. Perhaps it was not too late to heal our friendship.

Captain Wilkins lodged at the inn at Paddington and came to call the next morning. The clouds continued to wring their tears upon us.

After we had tea, Sarah picked up the tray and turned to Aunt Evelyn. "There was something I wanted to discuss with you, dear Aunt, about Father's menu. Would you come review the dishes Cook has suggested?" Sarah led the way from the room, and with a backwards glance and a quick wink, Aunt Evelyn followed.

Captain Wilkins's face lifted in a slight grin, and he pretended to pick a piece of lint from his pants. My throat felt suddenly tight. I did not want them to leave. I was not ready to be alone with Captain Wilkins. My heart fluttered a hundred different ways, not one of which was good.

"Miss Leah—" he began.

"It was very kind of you to escort us home, Captain," I cut in.

"Yes, well—"

"And please give my appreciation to your commander. It was very generous of him to grant your leave," I quickly said.

"It was my pleasure. The trip has worked to everyone's advantage in that I shall get to see my family for Christmas." He smiled, and his blue eyes twinkled. He tried again. "Miss Leah—"

I jumped out of my seat, halting his words once more, and moved to the window in front of the old oak tree. "Oh, I do hope you don't have to travel in the rain." I wrung my hands and felt like my lungs were collapsing inside my chest, making me fight for every breath.

And then Captain Wilkins moved and stood beside me! He reached for my hand, and I struggled to form a cohesive thought. His blue eyes were so kind, and he was very handsome. My cold hand felt nice in his warm ones. And for all that was nice, I could not think why it all felt so wrong.

He stroked his thumb across my fingers. "Miss Leah, before you turn completely pale and faint on me, let me put your mind at ease." He bent down and brought my eyes to meet his. "I am not going to propose to you."

My head jerked up, and I squeaked out, "You're not?"

He shook his head with a tender smile. "No."

"But . . ." I was not sure what I wanted to say, and my swirling confusion was not assisting me in forming any sort of coherent sentence. Captain Wilkins raised his free hand and placed a finger across my lips. His touch was not helping either. I pinched my mouth closed and concentrated on breathing through my nose.

"It's not that I do not want to propose." Captain Wilkins laughed softly and dropped his hand from my lips. "You are an amazing girl, and for a while I thought I may have had a chance." He looked at his hands grasping mine. "You see, as selfish as it may seem, I want my wife to cherish me. I want to be the one she looks at with loving eyes and pure devotion." He raised his eyes back to mine. "I've seen that look in your eyes, Miss Leah," his blond head shook, "but you were not looking at me."

"Oh," I breathed. I looked down at our hands and followed his movement as he lifted them to his lips. He placed a kiss, first on the back of one hand and then the other.

"I . . . I'm sorry," I stammered.

"Hush, dear girl." He offered a sincere smile. "It was an honor and a pleasure to know you, Miss Leah. And someday you will make someone very happy. I just hope it doesn't take him too long to figure that out."

Captain Wilkins released my hands, reclaimed his hat from the sofa, and walked out of the drawing room. I stood at the window and watched the rain continue to pour as the captain collected his horse and disappeared down the lane.

I just hope it doesn't take him too long to figure that out. My feelings must have been far more transparent than I had realized. I thought I had shielded my heart, wrapped it up so it could not be seen or recognized. But Captain Wilkins had seen through my defenses. He knew the chinks in my armor, but he could not know that the future he saw could never come to pass. Mrs. Ansley had made certain of that.

I turned and looked at the reaching branches of the oak tree. Rain drenched the tree as if assuring me that the elements would always win. No matter the depth of its roots or the elevation of its limbs, the tree was subject to the sun, the wind, and the rain. The struggling limbs could never grasp the small piece of heaven they reached for.

When I told Sarah about my audience with Captain Wilkins, she was pensive.

"The captain is a good man, Leah," Sarah said.

"Yes. He is. He was so valiant to escort us home. He has always been kind and attentive."

"He's handsome as well." Sarah smiled, and I nodded. "But?" she prodded.

"Do you remember when you told me about Mr. Dashel?" I sat down next to Sarah, but my eyes averted her face. "You described how you felt when you were with him." When I finally looked at my sister, her eyes held patience and understanding. "Captain Wilkins, he—he was good and kind . . ."

"But he didn't make you feel whole?" Sarah concluded.

"No," I answered simply. Sarah pulled me into a hug, holding me close in a warm embrace that I desperately needed. In Sarah's arms, I was finally able to release the guilt that had compounded because I could not love Captain Wilkins the way he deserved to be loved.

The rain continued through the following weeks, keeping me indoors and driving me to desperate boredom. Cousin Nora had readily accepted my apologies, and we began to correspond regularly. I had read two new novels, completed four samplers, and played the pianoforte poorly enough that Aunt Evelyn begged me to kindly stop.

So when the rain began to let up and Mrs. Ansley called with her daughter in tow, I welcomed the distraction—until she opened her mouth and I was reminded of the obnoxious honking geese. She asked after

Father's health, and as Sarah updated her on his recovery, Mrs. Ansley pinched her lips and kept looking at me sideways.

"Miss Leah," Mrs. Ansley chirped, "have you seen Mr. Brumley since your return?" The woman certainly did not mince words. She looked at me pointedly, waiting for a response.

"No," I said. Let the ornery woman think she had won. It did not matter now. "In fact, I did not realize the Brumleys had returned." Mrs. Ansley huffed. Obviously she did not believe me. "Aunt Evelyn has corresponded with Mrs. Brumley, but I have not had occasion to." Aunt Evelyn offered a convincingly bright smile.

"Hmmm." Mrs. Ansley pinched her lips so tight they really did look like the beak of a waterfowl.

I folded my hands in my lap and hoped my words warded off any further rebuke from the wretched woman.

Catherine began to share a new book she had read, but her mother cut her off sharply and instead elaborated on the four new dresses they had ordered to ensure Catherine would be in the height of fashion. After a half an hour they took their leave—but not before Mrs. Ansley cornered me and tersely reminded me of her callous threats.

Their visit made the rest of the day pass impossibly slow. My thoughts wandered to Mr. Brumley and when I might see him again. The Brumleys had remained at Landers Lodge through the Christmas holiday, and until Mrs. Ansley's visit, I had not heard any word of their plans to return to Derbyshire.

I waited a solid hour after the Ansleys' departure to question my aunt. "Did you know the Brumleys had returned home?" I asked, attempting to appear occupied by adjusting the sash on the curtains.

"In Mrs. Brumley's most recent correspondence, she may have mentioned they were returning to Riverton Park. I don't recall exactly," Aunt Evelyn answered evenly while she picked out a flaw from her needlework.

With slow, deliberate steps, I walked the circumference of the room. "Did the entire party return?"

"Hmm?" Aunt Evelyn lowered her sampler. She appeared bothered to answer my question.

"I just asked if the entire Brumley family had returned home? Perhaps Mrs. Brumley mentioned it in her letter?" I smiled in an attempt to make the forced conversation more natural.

"Leah," Aunt Evelyn scolded, "if you want to know what information I can share about Mr. Brumley, spit it out. This beating around the bush is maddening." She clucked her tongue and thrust her needle back into the fabric. "My dearly departed Mr. Clem used to say, 'Don't kill the hen when all you really want is an egg.'"

"I was simply wondering what news you had received," I said curtly.

Aunt Evelyn pursed her lips and grunted. I returned to the window.

When I was young, I would describe being nervous as having jitters in my belly. The things I felt when I believed Captain Wilkins might propose or the discomfort that I now experienced in Charles's presence—it was all very different. How does one differentiate between the aches and pains, the pulls and twists of one's insides? I concluded that nerves affect the belly, but when it comes to matters of the heart, my whole being became afflicted with a sort of shifting and tingles—a sensation that defies description. It was all-consuming but something to treasure rather than dread.

Inevitably, when I remembered my last dance with Charles and the way he held me as we moved with the music, my insides would shift and twist in a feeling that was quite welcome, and I was anxious to feel it again.

Dr. Hutchins eventually cleared Father to take dinner with the family and resume the majority of his regular activities. Cook prepared a celebratory meal, and we all shared in the contagious joy.

Ferrin continued tending to the estate, as Father was not quite ready for the task, and when we retired to the drawing room, the two discussed business. Father's pride in Ferrin's attentions to the tenants was evident, and I enjoyed watching Father's happiness filter through his smile.

Reading did not pacify me. I could not sit still. After my fifth circle around the drawing room, Sarah asked, "Shall I play the pianoforte? Then you might skip around the room instead of walking the carpet bare."

I glowered at my sister, and she simply smirked back.

"Better yet, just invite Mr. Brumley over, and they can share a dance," Aunt Evelyn offered with a culpable smile. "That should put an end to the brooding."

Aunt Evelyn had often been blunt, but my jaw hung open at her candid assertion.

"Leah, dear, is something bothering you?" Father lowered his reading glasses and set aside the ledger the men had been reviewing.

"No, Father. I've just been indoors too long. I'm making up for the lack of exercise." I meant to tease, but Father's face grew serious.

"No walk again today?" Father asked. "Doesn't that make three days in a row?" He turned towards Ferrin with a genuine look of concern.

"The weather hasn't been cooperating with my plans." I motioned towards the window.

Father humphed. "A little drizzle has never deterred you before. What's keeping you from your exercise, my dear? Are you sure you're feeling all right?"

"Yes, Father, I'm quite well," I tried to assure him. There was no need for him to worry. "Restlessness is my only ailment."

Ferrin coughed. I ignored him.

"I dare say the rain will dissipate tomorrow, so I am guaranteed a full day of exercise and sun," I offered with a smile. I could put on a happy show for Father. I was extremely happy for him. He still used the sling now and again when his shoulder felt sore or when he rode in the carriage. To see him recovered lifted my heart, and I almost felt whole.

Almost.

"I called at the Brumleys' today," Ferrin said, baiting me. "I wanted to give them an update on Father's recovery."

"How does Riverton Park fare?" Sarah asked, cheerily playing along.

"Mrs. Brumley was grateful to be home. Anxious to tend to her flowers." Ferrin leaned back in his chair.

"And how about Mr. Brumley?" Father asked. "I hope he is not still moping around."

"I only stayed briefly; thus it was hard to determine his temperament. He asked after the family and was cordial as always," Ferrin reported and flashed me a smile and a raised eyebrow.

And that was it. No more news came.

Every day that passed without Charles made me doubt whether or not I would ever feel entirely complete. I knew we could not be together—because of Mrs. Ansley and her promise—but I wondered about Charles, where he was, if he was happy.

Aunt Evelyn called at Riverton Park later in the week, but her report was barely more than an acknowledgment that Charles still lived and breathed.

"I sat with Rachel and Mrs. Brumley for almost an entire hour. Oh yes, and I did hear a horse outside, which I believed to be Mr. Brumley. He is not very social, you know." And that was the extent of her information.

Charles had almost kissed me again in his book room after we danced. I often wondered what might have happened if I'd let him. I asked myself this question many times and took comfort in my conclusion: I could not let Charles kiss me.

I loved him, but I needed to forgive him. Forgiveness had to come first. I could forgive him because I loved him. Yet I could not allow myself to ardently surrender my heart until I knew I had forgiven him completely. It was such a complex cycle, but one I had recounted so many times it was now ingrained in my conscious. Love equaled forgiveness; complete forgiveness equaled complete love.

My heart forgave Charles—my heart, my mind, my entire being. I forgave him for walking away that warm summer day. I forgave him for Father's accident. And I forgave him for making me love him. Clinging to his mistakes had hindered my own repentance. I needed to let go in order to allow both of us to be free.

As the days passed, new buds began to appear on the oak tree. In a few short months, it would be dressed with thousands of brilliant leaves. Rejuvenation took time, and I could finally look at the tree and see that it wasn't trying to reach heavenward. The oak was extending its branches to allow more buds to form and more leaves to grow. By expanding itself and sharing its splendor with the world, the oak brought a piece of heaven to the earth.

I wanted to grow like the tree. I wanted a bit of that paradise in my life. My roots were deep, my frame was willing, but Mrs. Ansley was a well-sharpened ax. Her threat cut me down and reminded me of my limits every time I thought I might attain happiness.

CHAPTER 35
Mr. Charles Brumley

❦

I THOUGHT IF I COULD occupy my time, the pain would somehow diminish. I rode daily through the forest, which reminded me of the times Leah and I climbed trees or went fishing. I tried to read some of my favorite works; however, my concentration faltered, and I found myself picturing Leah's speckled eyes smiling back at me. I missed those eyes.

Those months ago when Mr. Hastings had invited me into his office to recant his consent to court Leah, I was shocked. I tried to pry the reason from him. He shook his head and told me that a man could not reason with a woman's heart, and in this case Leah's heart lay elsewhere. When I insisted on speaking directly with Leah, Mr. Hastings politely refused, rebuking me as he would a son.

"Brumley," he had said, "trust me. You do not want to force a woman's hand in things such as this. Let patience be your companion, and in the end, all will turn out as it should."

His meaning was no clearer now than it was then. If I was patient, would Leah change her mind? Or I would see her lost to another and through patience find a companion of my own? Drat the old man and his assumed wisdom. My patience could only last so long.

Once the accident happened, my plight was hopeless. There had been moments when Leah looked at me and warm recollections of childhood passed between us. I told her I loved her right before confessing my crime. Timing had never been my forte.

Mrs. Clem called again at Riverton Park and updated Mother on Mr. Hastings's improving health. He regularly attended dinner with the family and was anxious for the approaching warmer weather so he could ride again. Mr. Hastings was near a full recovery, for which I was eternally grateful.

Mrs. Clem also confirmed that Captain Wilkins had escorted the family home but did not stay long. Surely, if there had there been an engagement, I would have heard, Leah's aunt would have shared. But Mrs. Clem did not mention it, and the Hastingses' servants, who had always been fiercely loyal, had not let word of an engagement slip. But short of a denial from Leah herself, I wondered if Captain Wilkins had won her heart.

Mother suggested hosting a dinner, but I adamantly refused. The life of a recluse suited me better. Mrs. Clem continued her regular visits, and Mrs. Ansley began to call more frequently with her poor daughter in tow.

After one such visit, Mother reported that we would be dining with the Ansleys the following evening. I offered every excuse I could muster, but my mother's insistence prevailed.

Mrs. Ansley zealously overindulged our small party. Mr. and Mrs. Harrison joined our two families, and what should have been a simple meal turned into a lavish feast. The cuisine was extraordinary, and while I complimented the Ansleys' cook, I also pitied her for the great pains such a meal must have required.

I sat beside Miss Ansley and across from her mother.

"We are so glad you have returned to Derbyshire, Mr. Brumley," Mrs. Ansley said. I acknowledged the servant setting the next course before me. "It has been such a dreary winter, but we can look forward to spring now that you have returned."

"I can hardly take credit for the changing seasons, madam." I took up my utensils and began to eat.

Mrs. Ansley's neck cricked to the side, and I glanced at the others around the table. My attention returned to my plate until I saw Mrs. Ansley twitch again. This time she accompanied her movement with a muffled cough.

Miss Ansley sighed and then asked, "Do you enjoy spring, Mr. Brumley?"

Spring. The mention of the season brought many fond recollections. However, as I reflected on those memories, they were laced with images of Leah—running through the blooming meadows, climbing budding trees, fishing, and exploring. The joy of the memories was tinged with pain, considering they now had an end. Leah's laughter ringing through the rain was no longer something I could look forward to. It only rang as an echo from my past.

I realized I had not answered the question. "It has been a long winter. The warmth of the spring sun will be most welcome."

The dinner conversation continued in this manner: Miss Ansley asking innocent questions as prodded by her mother while rich dishes were set before us. By the time dessert was served, I could only manage a few bites.

When the women departed, the gentlemen were happy company, and my stomach settled as we talked about business and horses.

We joined the ladies, and Mrs. Ansley's shrill voice disrupted the peace I had enjoyed with the men. She cawed over her daughter's newly acquired wardrobe, mortifying the girl. "Some may think that brighter tones are fashionable, but I have it on good authority that pastels and lace will be the rage this season." Mrs. Ansley offered a caustic laugh and waved her fan at Miss Ansley's pale-rose gown. Her eyes flicked to mine, then she turned her address back to Rachel and my mother. "Catherine is so modest when it comes to these things, but she really does have exceptional taste. Tell them, my dear, what was that novel you were reading the other day?" Mrs. Ansley scanned the room again.

"Mother, I'd rather—"

"Nonsense," Mrs. Ansley squawked, raising her eyebrows as she looked at me with a crooked smile. "Tell them."

It was easy to dismiss the presumptive ladies of the ton. Their tactics were preposterous and demeaning. Miss Ansley, however, remained innocent of any motive. Her manners were refined, her taste elegant, her conversation enlightening. Her problem was her mother. Mrs. Ansley's goals were obvious. She must have been ignorant of the fact that my heart was otherwise engaged.

I took a steeling breath and moved towards the women. "Miss Ansley, would you care to join me for a walk around the room?" The room was not large, so the request was rather absurd, but I could think of no other way to extricate Miss Ansley from her mother.

Miss Ansley would not bring her eyes to mine. She simply fell in step beside me, and we began our circle around the sofa.

"Mr. Brumley," she began, "do you remember when we danced at Landers Lodge and I told you that one day I would have the . . ." She lifted her chin and turned towards me. "The courage to disagree with my mother?" I smiled and stopped walking. She squared her shoulders and with a triumphant look said, "I think that time has finally arrived."

I couldn't have agreed more.

In mid-April, Fausett claimed to need a respite from Town and came to stay at Riverton Park. I welcomed the distraction his visit provided.

Fausett insisted we call upon the Hastings, and after waylaying his plans for a week, I could no longer find a viable excuse. I'd not seen Leah for almost four months, and my erratic heartbeat kept that fact in constant reminder.

Fausett always made easy conversation, and such was the case today. He asked after Mr. Hastings's health, complimented Mrs. Clem's needlework, and inquired after Miss Hastings's intended. At the mention of a fiancé, I scanned the room, searching Leah's face a little longer than the others. The neutrality in her expression gave nothing away.

Ferrin joined us and offered a welcome smile.

"How does Captain Wilkins fare? What news do you have of him?" Fausett probed. I stiffened at his question, and while I dreaded the answer, I silently thanked him for asking it. I would have to ask Cook to make her scrumptious trifle for dessert tonight. It was Fausett's favorite.

Miss Hastings looked towards Leah for an answer. Leah offered none, and after an awkward moment, Miss Hastings offered a subtle smile to Mr. Fausett. "Shortly after seeing us home, Captain Wilkins returned to Lincolnshire to spend Christmas with his family. He was very kind in his attentions towards us."

Ferrin moved his hand across his mouth, wiping away a grin. He cleared his throat. "Yes, Captain Wilkins is a good man, and I am indebted to him for returning my family safely to Astoria."

Fausett looked amused with this game and could not resist playing along. "And do you plan to see him again anytime soon?"

Leah's foot swung wildly beneath her skirts, and she again deferred to her siblings for an answer.

"Captain Wilkins did not tell us his plans. I did tell him how much I would enjoy seeing him at my wedding, but I'm not sure if he can acquire leave again so soon. I don't know how easily those types of affairs are managed." Miss Hastings turned to me. "Perhaps you could assist him as you did before, Mr. Brumley." She offered me a not-so-innocent smile. Leah and I had teased her relentlessly in our younger days. It appeared the time for retribution had arrived.

I opened my mouth to respond but found I had nothing to say on the matter. I rehashed the conversation quickly in my mind, only to discover that I knew nothing more about Captain Wilkins's role in the family than I had upon entering the house.

Leah practically leapt out of her seat. It startled Mrs. Clem, and she dropped her needlework, which Fausett bent over to retrieve.

"You are the epitome of generous," Mrs. Clem said, batting her eyes at Fausett as she accepted her embroidery from him. "Mr. Clem was always the perfect gentleman. Your manners are very similar to his."

My impatience yielded to anger. Their jesting at my expense reopened wounds that were far too raw. Miss Leah had moved to the window, and I was done. "I'm afraid my extended stay at Landers Lodge has left me with much to do. I pray you will excuse me."

Leah turned around abruptly. "You're leaving so soon."

It was not a question, and she looked perplexed by the notion. It caught me off guard. "Well . . . yes. I have business I must attend to."

"Before we can—call for tea?" Leah walked quickly to the bell pull. "You must have tea."

Ferrin smeared another smile off his lips.

Spending time with Leah would have been a pleasure, but I did not want an audience critiquing every word or sentence we shared. Fausett would harass me enough when we returned to Riverton Park.

"I thank you, Miss Leah, but I really must be going." I bowed and walked out of the room.

CHAPTER 36
Miss Leah Hastings

❧❀❧

I WANTED TO OPEN MY mouth to tell Charles that Captain Robert Wilkins meant nothing to me, but I could not form the words. Every time I saw my father or Ferrin or even my good Aunt Evelyn, Mrs. Ansley's threat opened the wounds I had worked so hard to bind.

The spark in Charles's eyes was more than friendship, and I was lying to myself to think my feelings were anything less than love. It was not dormant friendship that caused this war within. It was the rising tide of something more, something bigger and grander than I had ever experienced before. I raised my hand to my chest, trying to suppress the pain I felt when Charles no longer stood in the room. He collected his horse and then disappeared around the copse of trees at the end of the lane.

Mr. Fausett left shortly after, and another wearisome day passed.

The next morning I enjoyed an early ride, and upon returning to the house, I passed Jensen carrying the mail to Father's office. "Miss Leah." Jensen bowed his head.

"Good morning, Jensen," I said. "Anything from Nora?"

"Not today, ma'am."

After changing out of my riding habit and collecting a favorite book from the library, I joined Aunt Evelyn in the drawing room. Father entered only a minute after.

"Leah, where is your sister?" he asked.

"Have you checked her room? I have yet to see her this morning," I answered.

Father walked to the wall and tugged on the bell pull. He turned towards the door when a servant arrived. "Please ask Miss Hastings to join us in the drawing room."

Aunt Evelyn and I exchanged a questioning look.

"Father, what's going on?" I asked.

He waved a letter in front of his face. "It seems we are to expect a visitor." Aunt Evelyn shrugged in ignorance, and I looked back at my father. "One Mr. William Dashel will arrive tomorrow morning." Father grinned.

Sarah's time with Aunt and Uncle Barnes had been cut short. Father had given permission for Uncle Barnes to speak on his behalf, yet when Sarah left posthaste to join us at Landers Lodge, Mr. Dashel had not yet found an opportunity to ask for Sarah's hand. Mr. Dashel was now coming to meet with Father.

"Leah! Stop staring out the window." Sarah waved her hand frantically. "Mr. Dashel might see you."

I complied and sat in the chair next to the sofa.

Sarah grinned wide. "The cut of that gown really does highlight your figure."

"Thank you," I replied.

"But stop slouching." Sarah reached over and pressed her palm against my back.

And thus it went for an hour. Sarah doling out praise then snapping like a turtle at the smallest infraction. Aunt Evelyn was humming too loud, and my hairpins were askew—until the next moment when Aunt's choice of colors were brilliant and my input on the menu was invaluable. It was difficult to follow Sarah's morphing emotions.

My own heart was in such a muddle that I understood her anxiety and tried to be patient, but my reserve was wearing thin. Thank goodness Mr. Dashel's delay was only temporary. His appearance pushed Sarah's temperament to exuberance.

Jensen introduced the man, and Mr. Dashel entered the drawing room with a grin spread wide across his face. From Sarah's description of him, I knew I would like her intended, but I was pleased to find that my first impression mirrored hers. It spoke peace to my soul that this would be the man my sister would marry.

Mr. Dashel had honey-colored hair, and his eyes were a combination of gold and green. I could not dispute that he was handsome, and his pleasant personality added to his charm.

After tea, we decided to stroll to the bridge downstream. Aunt Evelyn agreed to join our small excursion. A chill rose with the evening air, and as we turned back towards the house, Ferrin approached on his horse. Introductions were made, and Ferrin joined our party, handing off his horse to the groom.

"Where are you staying?" Sarah asked Mr. Dashel.

"The inn at Paddington," Mr. Dashel replied.

"Nonsense," Ferrin interjected. "I shall send a man to collect your things. I insist you stay at Astoria."

"If you are sure it is not an inconvenience?"

Ferrin slapped him on the shoulder with a happy smile. "Not at all."

Sarah's cheeks transformed to a very becoming shade of red.

After dinner the men lingered, and Sarah paced in agitated circles around the drawing room.

"Shall I play the pianoforte so you can skip around the room instead of wearing the carpet bare?" I teased her with the same line she had employed on me.

Sarah snapped her head towards me, ready to defend herself, but her retort was cut off when the men entered. Her apprehension transformed to happiness when Mr. Dashel crossed the room and greeted her. Father watched this too, and when I caught his smiling eyes, he gave me a quick wink.

After only thirty minutes, Father suggested we retire early.

"Mr. Clem always said, 'The early bird gets the worm,'" Aunt Evelyn said as she drifted into the hallway.

"Dashel, why don't you join Ferrin and me tomorrow as we check on our tenants," Father suggested.

Mr. Dashel bowed. "It would be my pleasure." He wished Sarah a good evening and moved to follow Father out the door.

Sarah's smile slipped as she watched him exit, and then her eyes fell to the floor.

"Oh, I almost forgot." Father poked his head back into the room after a moment and offered a mischievous smile. "Sarah, Mr. Dashel would like to speak to you in private. He is waiting in my study."

Sarah flitted to the door with a renewed hope in her eyes. I followed her from the room and walked with my father to the bottom of the stairs. We both turned and watched Sarah place her hand over her heart before she entered Father's study.

"Dear Leah, I hope one day you will know how much joy a parent receives when they see their children content," Father mused.

My enthusiasm for my sister bubbled in my limbs. Father and I climbed the stairs together with wide, happy grins.

"So you approve of Mr. Dashel?" I asked.

"Wholeheartedly," Father consented. "It's obvious he adores Sarah, and he will make her happy." We reached the landing, and with a sobering expression, Father took my hands in his. "Leah, it has been difficult for me to watch the gloom diminish your vivacity for life. Something has extinguished your usual joy." He shook his head sorrowfully. "I'm not sure what it is, but I hope you discover how to chase away the cobwebs so that you too can be happy, my dear." Father's crinkled eyes stared into mine. The corner of his mouth turned up, and he kissed my cheek. He left me standing there as he entered his room.

Finding happiness was not the problem. I knew that the one thing— or rather, one person—that could make me happy was just down the lane. It was the path to attain that happiness that continued to elude me.

CHAPTER 37
Mr. Charles Brumley

❧

AN ENGAGEMENT CELEBRATION. THAT WAS all the invitation stated. No names, no explanation. My heart sank with despair. I needed answers, and in the parlor sat the one woman who might be able to provide them.

Mother and Mrs. Clem moved to rise upon our entrance, but I held up my hand and insisted they remain seated. "We just wanted to offer a quick hello," I said.

Mother lifted her brow, and Mrs. Clem harrumphed.

"That color highlights your youthful countenance," Fausett said to Mrs. Clem as he bowed over her hand.

She batted her eyelashes. "Blue was one of Mr. Clem's favorites."

"And you look lovely as always, Mrs. Brumley."

Mother waved off Fausett's praise and gave me a look of indignation.

My emotions could not handle small talk, so I jumped right in. "We were privileged to receive an invitation to dine at Astoria, Saturday next." I braced myself. "How lucky to be included in such a happy occasion."

Fausett and I had both tried to dissect the invitation that had arrived four days ago. There was rumor that Mr. Dashel was in town, but I had not been able to confirm that the celebration was on account of him and Miss Hastings. A clogged flue had caused a devastating fire for one of my tenants, and the previous two days had been consumed with acquiring new lodging and supplies for the young family. It constantly plagued me that I had not been able to verify the rumors.

"Yes," Mrs. Clem said. "It has caused quite a commotion in our home, as we weren't expecting the gentleman to express his desires so soon. We only received word of his visit the day prior." Mrs. Clem plucked something off her dress and clasped her hands in her lap. She pressed her lips together and watched me squirm.

I shifted uneasily beneath her gaze while my mind stumbled to think of another approach.

"Has the couple set a date for the wedding?" Mr. Fausett asked.

"Indeed, they have. Next month," Mrs. Clem said. "They are very anxious to be done with the entire ordeal."

"Astoria must be bustling with preparations," Mother said. "Please, Evelyn, let the girls know that I would be happy to assist in any way possible."

The two women beamed with their little game, and my patience wore thin. Forget decorum. I needed answers. I cleared my throat and tried to keep my voice level. "The invitation was vague at best. Who exactly is engaged?"

Mrs. Clem grinned mischievously and answered, "Leah is very happy." My heart sunk, and my limbs froze. Fortunately, my immobilized position allowed me to witness the wink Mrs. Clem granted Fausett before she continued. "She couldn't be more pleased that Sarah's engagement is finally secure."

My shoulders fell, and I finally exhaled while Mrs. Clem batted her eyelashes and offered an unrepentant grin.

Jensen met us at the door, dressed in Astoria's finest livery.

"Mrs. Brumley, Mr. Brumley, Mr. Fausett, and Miss Brumley." He bowed and waved us inside. "We have been expecting you. The party is assembled in the drawing room."

"Thank you, Jensen." Mother moved past the familiar butler and led us inside.

Before we reached the gathering, I heard the shrill voice of Mrs. Ansley. I closed my eyes and paused in the doorway.

"Come on, old chap. It's not that bad." Fausett slapped me on the back. "Remember, Miss Leah is through those doors." Fausett nudged me forward.

He was right. Whatever pains Mrs. Ansley may cause, they were worth it to spend the evening in Leah's presence. With a restorative breath, I entered the room.

Leah's eyes met mine. Warm and happy at first; then something changed. The confident girl I knew retreated, and in her place stood a star-tled fawn. She rapidly blinked, and her mouth twitched, uncertain if she should smile or frown. Leah stood and stared, and I stupidly did the same.

"Ah, Mr. Brumley." Mrs. Ansley walked towards me. Her hand firmly grasped her daughter's wrist as she towed her along. "We are so pleased you could make it. Aren't we, darling?" She curtsied alongside Miss Ansley and gave an awkward grunt.

I pressed my eyes closed again and after a deep breath acknowledged the duo.

"Quite a celebration." Mrs. Ansley motioned to the room. "Maybe this happy event will serve as a prelude to more similar announcements. Hmm?" Her eyes widened, and her lips pinched together. The evening had scarce begun, and I was already tired of Mrs. Ansley's antics.

"If you'll excuse me." I bowed quickly. "I must congratulate the happy couple."

Fausett mirrored my departure, and together we moved to acquaint ourselves with Mr. Dashel. We stepped away from the Ansley women, and Fausett whispered under his breath, "That woman is determined, Brumley. You had better be careful, or her words may prove prophetic."

We maneuvered behind the sofa and skirted towards the fireplace, where Miss Hastings stood with her intended. I scoffed. "Come now, Fausett. Miss Ansley is a dear girl. She's handsome—"

"Yes, very handsome," Fausett acknowledged.

I stopped and rolled my eyes. "She has a kind heart and is quite talented."

"So you do notice the girl?" Fausett asked.

"Of course. Who wouldn't?" We moved forward and waited behind Mr. and Mrs. Harrison to offer our congratulations. "However, there are two reasons I will never court Miss Ansley. First, I could never survive being the son-in-law of that woman." I jerked my head to where Mrs. Ansley stood. "Second, as you well know, my affections are elsewhere. Now then, let's give our congratulations to someone whom I would happily call family."

CHAPTER 38
Miss Leah Hastings

❧

AFTER MR. BRUMLEY ENTERED THE room, my mind whirled. Our eyes met, and everything I had wanted and hoped for and dared to dream washed over me at once. The emotion was solid and frightening because it was out of my control. My feelings did not matter. My heart was but an afterthought.

Mrs. Ansley approached Charles, machinating her plan to ensnare him to her daughter. 'Twas a pity, for I liked Catherine. If she indeed married Charles, those warm feelings were bound to dissolve with my jealousy.

The barrage of sentiment left me feeling weak, and I forced myself to step aside so I could bind my emotions up once more. Settling on the sofa, I deliberately monitored my breathing—a slow breath in, a long breath out. My pulse returned to normal, and my walls expanded to take in my surroundings.

Sarah and Mr. Dashel stood content near the fireplace. Father's voice boomed with laughter as he visited with Mr. Ansley. From behind I heard another voice, one I knew well. It was Mr. Brumley talking in a quiet whisper.

"Come now, Fausett. Miss Ansley is a dear girl. She's handsome—"

"Yes, very handsome," Fausett agreed.

Then Mr. Brumley said something about her kind heart and her talents.

"So you do notice the girl?" Fausett asked.

"Of course. Who wouldn't?" Charles replied.

My walls crumbled on top of me. Who wouldn't notice Catherine? Beautiful, talented, and kind. There was nothing more to be said, nothing more to be done.

"Leah?" Aunt Evelyn called from somewhere beyond my coherence. "Leah?" I raised my head to see her watching me, her brow creased with concern. "You look as though you've seen a ghost." She moved to sit beside me. "Are you quite all right?"

"No. I mean, yes. I mean . . . I just need a minute." A slow breath in, a long breath out. I pushed myself up from the sofa and walked to the windows. Shadows cloaked the oak tree now. Darkness would always put an end to the day. Darkness would win.

"Miss Leah." Mr. Fausett stepped up beside me with a drink in his hand. I acknowledged him with a pathetic attempt at a smile. "I've just met your future brother-in-law."

I wrapped my arms across my chest. "Yes, Mr. Dashel will be a welcome addition to the family." I stared out the window at nothing. "Will you be staying long in Derbyshire, Mr. Fausett?"

"I had only planned on staying for a couple of weeks. But then came the happy announcement. I did not realize that the wedding would take place so soon." He shrugged. "Perhaps I will extend my stay."

"Sarah wants a simple ceremony. No pomp. She only wants to be wed to the man she loves." I looked at Mr. Fausett. "Would you suggest a delayed ceremony in order to accommodate a more elaborate celebration?"

"Not at all." Mr. Fausett held his glass as if to offer a toast. "A love match is a rare thing. If they are determined to be married, they should post the banns and be wed at once. They are a very fortunate couple indeed."

"Yes, they are," I said, but my stomach pinched uncomfortably. My gaze returned to the window. There was nothing to observe; darkness had taken its hold.

Mr. Fausett stood silently beside me. After a few quiet moments, he tilted his head and asked, "Miss Leah, are you still determined to learn how to shoot a bow?"

I was touched that he had remembered my simple desire from all those months ago. "Yes," I answered. "I am."

"Could I persuade you to allow me to teach you? At, say, ten o'clock on Monday?"

"I would like that, Mr. Fausett. Thank you." Father's laughter rang again, and I turned back to face the room. I spied Charles standing near the pianoforte talking to Miss Ansley. "Will Mr. Brumley mind?" I asked. "I wouldn't want him to begrudge me for occupying your time."

Mr. Fausett took a drink. "Brumley is my host, but he does not dictate my schedule. Besides, I am quite determined that you should learn archery. I believe if you are determined to do something, you should always follow through."

Mr. Fausett moved around the sofa to amuse my dear aunt. Mr. Brumley lowered his head and whispered in Catherine's ear. She blushed prettily and smiled at him.

Charles and Catherine. I suppose it was inevitable. He was the prize Mrs. Ansley had sought, and now she could claim victory.

I blinked back my tears. Mrs. Ansley had won.

CHAPTER 39
Mr. Charles Brumley

FINALLY, IT WAS DONE; I had convinced Miss Ansley that her mother did not deserve to run her life. We both acknowledged that Mrs. Ansley had been playing matchmaker on our behalf. Miss Ansley was embarrassed, but her admission allowed her to realize how much she detested the prospect of life determined by her mother.

She tiptoed around a full confession, no doubt afraid she would wound my ego. If only she could know that slighting me was the first step in standing up to her mother. She unabashedly professed her feelings for Ferrin.

Pleased with this admission, I pressed her to tell her mother.

"Oh, but I couldn't," Miss Ansley said. "Mother would never approve."

"But remember, Miss Ansley, 'tis your life, not your mother's. What is your father's opinion on the matter?"

"Father has always held the Hastingses in high regard." Miss Ansley's eyes grew wide, and she quickly put a hand on my arm. "Not that he doesn't think highly of you as well, Mr. Brumley."

I laughed and placed my hand on top of hers.

She colored again and said, "It's just that Mr. Hastings, well, he makes me laugh."

"May I be the first to congratulate you on your newfound cheek," I said.

"It is time, isn't it?" she asked.

"Yes. It is," I said, and relief coursed through my veins.

There was something about watching Mr. Dashel and Miss Hastings. Their glow spread through the entire room. Their manners were easy, their attention devoted. They were in love, and I was a jealous fool. I wanted to share meaningful glances. I wanted to be the recipient of simple touches warmed with love. I wanted to satisfy the yearning that encased my soul, the feeling that had nestled there years ago and never surrendered. I wanted Leah to be mine.

I excused myself from Miss Ansley and joined Leah in her vigil near the window. She stared at the blackened sky. The darkness amplified her profile. Her cheeks were pale, and her expression lacked her usual playful demeanor.

"Good evening, Miss Leah."

"Hello, Charles." She turned and smiled.

My heart warmed at the familiarity of that smile until I realized it was stilted. When I looked in her eyes, I knew something was amiss. The speckles within stared back, but the light was absent.

"I guess I won't be able to call you that much longer," she said, and her smile fell.

"What do you mean?" I angled my chest between Leah and the window, providing a private nook for our exchange. "You must always call me Charles."

Her eyes fell to the windowsill. "That would not be entirely proper, Mr. Brumley." She attempted to say my name with a teasing lilt, but her efforts fell flat.

I thought we had settled this issue, and I could not make sense of her words. "Leah . . ." I began.

She raised a finger in reprimand. "Miss Leah."

She gasped as I grabbed her hand in both of mine. I encased her fingers in my own and adjusted my body to ensure our hands were shielded from prying eyes. "Leah. *Miss Hastings*," I teased. "What is this about?" My heart raced. I tenderly cradled her fingers in my own, and she did not move.

Her eyes danced between our hands, and her breath froze. The color in her cheeks drained further.

"Are you unwell?" I asked. I dropped one hand and started to lead her to a chair.

She grabbed my wrist. "No, Mr. Brumley. I—I am fine. Or . . . I will be."

"We need to talk, Leah," I said. "It's been too long, and there is so much to say."

"It's okay, Mr. Brumley. I already know." Leah forced the corners of her mouth to turn upward. "It's always been difficult for us to say good-bye." She blinked rapidly and looked away.

"Good-bye?" I mouthed the words.

Leah squeezed my hand. "Thank you for all the memories, Mr. Brumley. I wish you many more." Leah gasped and released my hand to cover her mouth. Moisture began pooling in her eyes.

What was going on? Why was she talking about good-bye when I wanted to talk about new beginnings? Leah's eyes used to light up when I entered a room. Her mouth would turn up into a smile, and it was better than coming home. Yet here she stood, talking about good-bye. "Leah," I took a stilling breath. "Miss Leah, I do not wish to discuss good-byes; they are far too somber."

"Mr. Brumley, you and I both know it cannot be any other way." Her voice caught as she continued. "An engagement is a reason for celebration." She bent her head, and gravity pulled a single tear from her eyes to the floor. She blinked rapidly and quickly swiped a finger under her lashes to clear away the moisture. "It will be okay, Mr. Brumley. Marriage was bound to happen for one of us."

And suddenly it all clicked. This *was* good-bye. She was following in Sarah's footsteps. Leah planned to marry Captain Wilkins.

My mouth hung open as I slowly absorbed the truth.

"No hard feelings, Mr. Brumley." Leah choked on the words as they tumbled from her lips. She leaned close as if she meant to kiss my cheek, but before she closed the distance, she pulled back and put her hand on my arm. "Good-bye." Her voice broke on a sob, and she hurried away.

CHAPTER 40
Miss Leah Hastings

❦

MY PREVIOUS DEJECTION WAS NOTHING compared to the miserable gloom now resting upon me. I thought Charles had been interested in courting because we got along well together. We could easily share a roof and pass many a happy day. Miss Ansley was a pretty face but lacked the wit and candor that would ignite Mr. Brumley's personality. Yet they were to be married.

Sleep would not come that night. I tossed and turned, twisting my bed sheets into a jumble. I finally rose and saw that the clouds had dispersed. The moon smiled down upon my window. I hoped a stroll on the veranda would calm the burning that continued to melt my insides.

I wrapped my cloak around my nightdress, donned my slippers, and made my way through the house to let myself silently out into the brisk night. I shivered in the cold, grateful for something other than ache and longing to penetrate my being.

Completing my second circle around the perimeter of the patio, I turned towards the house and was startled when Father stepped from the shadows.

"My dear Leah, what has brought you out at this time of night?" Father's eyes were full of questions to which I had no answers. He opened the door and ushered me inside. "Come, child. Let's go to the library and see if we can chase away our ghosts together."

Father slowly bent over the wood box and laid two pieces of wood on the glowing ashes.

"Father, please let me."

"Nonsense." He waved me away. "What a useless creature I am if I cannot even light a small fire." He chuckled. "From warm ashes nonetheless."

With minimal effort, Father pumped the billows, and the flame quickly reappeared. I tucked myself into a large chair facing the fire and pulled my cloak around my shoulders, waiting for the warmth of the fire to envelop me.

"There now." After dusting his hands and replacing the tools, Father sat in a nearby chair. "Quite a sight, the full moon."

"Yes, it's beautiful." I sighed.

"But?" Father turned his eyes on me.

We sat silent for several minutes until I asked, "What do you remember of Mother's passing?"

If my father was shaken by my question, I could not tell. He braced his chin against his fingers and stared at the dancing flames in the hearth.

Without looking my direction, he responded, "It's a night I have tried to push from my mind. Yet the memory will forever be emblazoned upon me." He finally pulled his eyes from the fire and turned them to me. "When I think of your dear mother, I choose to reflect upon happier times, yet when I think back on that night, I have solace in the fact that it was what your mother wanted."

"What she wanted?" I repeated incredulously.

Father nodded. "She had been so ill, and she must have known the end was drawing near. Her maid thought me mad in my grief to not call Dr. Hutchins to return. Even threatened call him herself. Yet how could I defy my wife's last wishes?" Father choked on the words, and his eyes dampened with the memory.

"Her wishes?" My voice cracked, and I waited with shaky breath for him to say something, to clarify, to tell me that Mother knew what was happening.

"Yes, she even wrote it down—a will of sorts." His lips quirked. "I think she knew I would waffle in the end and thought having it on paper would make it more official. Your mother always knew she was my weakness." He gasped in a short, staggered breath.

"Father." I lowered my feet to the floor and leaned forward in my chair. "Are you telling me Mother asked you not to call the doctor?"

"She outright forbade it." He pressed his lips into a tight line, and a strangled sob escaped.

"Why did you not tell me? All these years . . . I wondered." My whisper fell away.

"Wondered?"

My lower lip trembled, and I told him all. "I was there, Father. I snuck into Mother's dressing room. I saw Louisa beg you to call the doctor, and you refused. And I—I never knew why."

"Oh, my dear Leah." Father reached forward and cradled both of my hands. "Why did you not say something before? You must have thought me so callous all this time." His head shook sorrowfully, and he looked at me with such sadness.

"Father, I never doubted you. I knew you loved her, and perhaps it was my childish naivety, but in my eyes nothing was amiss." I squeezed his hands. "Until . . ." Our eyes met. Father lowered his head for me to continue. "Until Mrs. Ansley threatened me," I concluded.

"What?" Father's voice returned at full volume, and he shot to his feet. "Threatened you how?" He stood tall, looming above me. His eyes filled with rage, and I shrank back in the chair. The tender reflections of my mother were gone, replaced with burning anger. My eyes grew wide, my lips trembled, and my father's face softened. Sternly he asked again, "Leah, how has Mrs. Ansley threatened you?"

I looked down at my hands squeezed together, took a fortifying breath, and turned back to my father. "She—she told me I was to stay away from Mr. Brumley. That I was not to encourage his suit, and if I did not heed her . . ." I paused, unsure if I should continue.

Flames from the fire cast flickering light on Father's clenched jaw. "Go on."

"She claimed to have proof that you refused to call Dr. Hutchins. She said if you had, Mother could have been saved. She threatened to expose you and ruin us all."

"Vile woman!" Father spat. He walked over and placed his hands on the mantel. He cursed under his breath and turned back towards me. "What right does she have threatening you?" His voice was rough with rage, but I knew his accosting anger was not directed towards me.

"She said . . ." I paused then realized I could not hold in this secret any longer. "She said that if it were known, there would be social as well as spiritual repercussions. She even hinted that you could go to trial." I scrambled to my feet and took a step towards him. "And while I am certain it would not have come to that, I did fear for Sarah and Ferrin. And for your honor."

I felt a release at finally sharing this burden, yet I realized for me to believe Mrs. Ansley meant my conviction in my father was lacking.

I caused the pain that I was trying to prevent. "I have betrayed you, believing her lies. I'm so sorry, Father. I should have come directly to you."

Father stormed to the window. The fire crackled brightly, contrasting the dismal gray that had settled between us. "You don't care for Captain Wilkins, do you?" he asked without turning around.

I wrung my hands again. "He is a kind and good man, and I had thought that perhaps we would suit. But . . ."

Father turned around, and his eyes smiled at me. I started in surprise, his face the opposite of what I had anticipated. "But your heart belongs to another?" he guessed.

"I believe so," I cried out, my eyes filling with tears.

Father opened his arms. I ran to him.

"There, there, child." He stroked my head as I cried into his shirt. "Don't give another thought to ornery Mrs. Ansley. I shall deal with her. But first I need to speak to Mr. Brumley. It seems we've had a misunderstanding."

I sniffed my tears dry and pulled back to look at my father. "I'm afraid it may be too late. I think he and Miss Ansley may have an understanding."

Father's laughter rumbled through his chest. "Miss Ansley? Oh, come now, Leah. I've seen the way Brumley looks at you. He's been smitten for years. When he asked to court you, I told him it was about time."

"Oh, Father." I raised my hand to my mouth and shook my head.

Father laughed again. "You were the one I could not decipher. I guessed you harbored feelings for Brumley, but I never knew for sure. When you told me Captain Wilkins had won your affection, I assumed I had misjudged." He placed his large hand on my shoulder. "Brumley loves you. Of that I am sure."

I placed my hand atop my father's. "Do you think he will forgive me for being so stubborn and blind?"

"I think he can only claim the same folly. If forgiveness is what he lacks, we will have to send him a few letters to expand his understanding of the principle."

I dropped my hands and stepped back. "Letters?"

My father's eyes held an answer that he did not reveal. Instead, he just looked at me.

"As in unsigned letters? Citing scripture or clergyman?" I clarified.

"I have another reference from Lord Herburt of Cherbury. Although it seems it was not necessary."

I turned my back on my father and faced the fire. "You sent them?" The question died on the warm air between us because we both knew the answer.

"Leah, I was the one who had been shot, but you seemed to harbor enough hatred for the both of us. If I did not blame Brumley, there was no reason for you to."

I looked at Father again. "I thought they were from him." I tried to explain. "At first they just made me more angry." I smiled. The wobbly scrawl, my father's love of scripture. It made sense.

Father chuckled. "I was afraid of your wrath. That's why I left them unsigned."

"But how did you deliver them to my room?"

"I can't reveal all of my secrets now, can I?"

My frozen heart began to thaw, and hope began to snip the strings that had restricted me for so long.

"What changed, Leah? I could sense it, but I could not place the reason behind your transformation."

"It was the third note you sent. 'We forgive to the extent that we love.'"

Father narrowed his eyes.

I looked at the ground and then returned his gaze with a smile. "I realized I loved Mr. Brumley."

With my admission, Father opened his arms, and I ran to him again.

CHAPTER 41
Mr. Charles Brumley

❦

"SHE ALL BUT TOLD ME that her future was with Captain Wilkins," I explained to Fausett.

"Gads, Brumley. You invited him to your home. You must not be entirely uninterested in the man." Fausett was kind enough to remind me of my missteps.

"I thank you yet again for your not-so-subtle reminder of another of my many blunders. May I request that you write all of my shortcomings down so rather than your constant reprimand, you could produce a running tally of my faults? I'd prefer a memorandum over your ceaseless prattle."

"Not a bad idea," Fausett mused. "It could be a continuous list so I could simply add each new transgression as it occurs."

"Scoundrel."

"Very well." Fausett stood. "On my honor, Brumley, Miss Leah is not to be engaged to the captain!"

"She all but told me so herself."

"Miss Leah told you she was going to marry Captain Wilkins?"

"What she said was that we should no longer address each other by our Christian names for it would be improper when one of us would soon be married. Then she said that good-byes were always difficult." My heart clenched at the recollection.

"Sounds to me like she did not want to say good-bye—to you."

"Yet she did."

"Did it ever occur to you that perhaps you misunderstood?" Fausett asked, and I heaved a labored sigh. "As I have already explained, Mrs. Clem told me—in no uncertain terms—that Captain Wilkins would not be renewing his interest in Miss Leah. She said the two parted as friendly acquaintances."

"You also said that Mrs. Clem told you that since Captain Wilkins's departure, Leah has been moping and depressed," I reminded him.

"No, I said since she returned home from Landers Lodge, which is an entirely different distinction. When she left Landers Lodge, she left you, Brumley, not the captain."

"It's no use, Fausett. I don't think I could bear her rejection again." I sunk into my chair.

Fausett scoffed his disagreement then said, "Well, in that case, I feel it best to inform you that I have an appointment with Miss Leah tomorrow."

I stiffened at his cavalier attitude but did not betray the annoyance we both knew I felt. I managed to keep my voice impartial. "And how did you arrange that?"

"I simply extended an invitation." He gave an unrepentant shrug.

My jaw tensed, but I refused to show him how flustered I was.

He laughed and said, "If you recall, I promised Miss Leah I would teach her archery. You, of course, are welcome to join us." He sighed. "However, I must admit I will not rue your obstinacy. I would very much enjoy instructing Miss Leah in the particulars of stance and position, as she will no doubt need some sort of tutelage to perfect her form."

"Blasted, Fausett!" He knew exactly how to rile me. "She is a lady."

"A single, *eligible* lady from what I understand." He resumed his cocky smirk.

I growled, and Fausett offered his hearty laugh again.

"It's a lesson, my friend. I simply aspire to be the perfect tutor." Fausett waved his arms wide.

I desperately wanted to hit his grinning jaw.

Fausett sobered. "The elder Miss Hastings has expressed a desire to learn as well. Since Mr. Dashel departed this morning, I suppose I could defer Miss Leah's training to you and help her elder sister." He dramatically sighed again. "It would be a sacrifice, to be sure—one I suppose I could make for an old friend."

I would like to think my intimidating scowl swayed Fausett, but more likely it was his plan all along. After a few calming breaths, I uncurled my clenched fists and asked, "When and where are these lessons to take place?"

"The Misses Hastings have agreed to ten o'clock tomorrow. I was hoping you might coordinate the where?"

My lips turned up in a smile. "I know the perfect place."

I stood in our secluded alcove, remembering the many times Miss Leah and I had defended our retreat in the trees from imaginary louts. Today the only thing she had to be fearful of was the bumbling fool I would make of myself.

I ran a hand through my hair and returned to setting the targets. Fausett and I had enlisted the servants' help in hauling the awkward bundles from Riverton Park earlier in the morning. We had delivered two targets, a table for the equipment, and another small table with four chairs. Mr. Fausett had used his charm on Cook and convinced her to prepare a last-minute picnic as well.

Counting off thirty paces, I walked away from the marks and fashioned a shooting line with a piece of rope. I readjusted the equipment—again—between the two rows.

I blew out a breath. I was a mess.

Fausett was taking his time gathering the ladies from the house, no doubt bantering and teasing smiles from them. An opening through the trees did not reveal their location, and I paced the shooting line for the third time.

My absence from Leah had further confirmed my affection for her. I fingered the blunted arrows and tried to calm my racing heart. I could not wait to see her. Fausett could rankle, but I knew he was an ally. He would draw Sarah away, and I would finally have an opportunity to speak with Leah alone. The idea filled me with dread and an inundating burst of anticipation.

I had confessed to Miss Leah my part in her father's accident. We had never spoken of it further. After we danced in my book room, she had said, "We forgive to the extent that we love." I had assumed the phrase was a psalm, yet upon researching the matter, I could not discover a verse with the exact verbiage. It bothered me. First, because I had not been able to determine where the adage was from. And second, the words themselves had given me great pause. After Leah shared the passage, her eyes turned light and happy, and she told me she had forgiven me. Then she walked away once again.

Her forgiveness was paramount. Raking guilt had consumed me for weeks, and I was grateful for her mercy. Yet in the passage she cited, forgiveness was tied to love. Could love perhaps have been the catalyst for her exoneration?

That night, my intention was to kiss her. She had to know, to realize what I was about to do, and then she stepped away. Her reaction was not one of surprise, yet it was a rejection. My heart felt spurned and raw, and then she recited a sonnet about love.

I would never understand her. I had tried to give her time and space, but we needed to talk. And for me, that moment could not come fast enough.

I picked a bow from the table we had positioned between the two targets and nocked an arrow on the bowstring. My boots shifted beneath my shoulders, and I postured my body sideways before taking aim. Drawing in a deep breath, I pulled the bowstring taut and tried to relax, to focus solely on the target. My mind flashed with visions of bewitching brown eyes and soft sweet lips. Another breath and I released.

The arrow flew and hit the bottom right corner of the target. It hung there for mere seconds before falling to the ground. If my nerves did not settle, I would not be an adequate instructor.

I nocked another arrow and adjusted my stance. The breaths that should have been calm were short and uneven. The second arrow flew wide and missed the target completely.

"Blasted—" I bit back the rest of the curse threatening to escape and shook my head. How could I expect to win the heart of a spirited woman if I could not control my nerves and rein them in for a proper hit on the target?

Determined for redemption with the bow, which I subconsciously related to redemption with Leah, I nocked a third arrow. One, two, three breaths. My heartbeat slowed, and I pulled the bowstring tight. Adjusting to the left, I narrowed my eyes on the center of the target.

A crashing noise in the trees pulled my attention from my pursuit, and my heart sped again at the unexpected interruption.

Admiral loped into the clearing and began barking incessantly. I sighed in exasperation and turned to evaluate my target once more. The dog continued to yap at me, and I could not concentrate.

"What, Admiral?" I snapped, lowering the bow and turning towards him.

No sooner was I facing the canine than he jumped at me and throttled me to the ground. The whole scene was reminiscent of the nightmare with Leah's father.

"Get off me, you infuriating beast!" I growled and shoved Admiral away.

He barked three or four more times then scampered off. My head pounded from the tackle, and I rubbed a hand over my eyes to push away the pain.

I heard a muted giggle and turned to see I had an audience. Fausett's eyes were wide with shock, and Miss Hastings looked scandalized. Miss Leah covered her mouth with her hand; it was from her that the laughter came. She valiantly tried to contain it, but little bursts sputtered out unintended. Although my head throbbed, I realized the ridiculousness of my situation, and my lips involuntarily twisted into a suppressed grin.

"Brumley, that is no way to greet these lovely ladies," Fausett said.

"Haven't I always told you I have rotten timing?" At my reference to timing, Leah's laughter erupted. My face split into a wide smile, and I sat in the dirt, admiring one particularly lovely lady.

CHAPTER 42
Miss Leah Hastings

❧❦❧

Mr. Fausett came to collect Sarah and me, but he would not reveal our destination. We knew we were to be shooting, and I was glad Sarah had agreed to come so Aunt Evelyn would not have to serve as chaperone. Aunt Evelyn was fond of Mr. Fausett and would no doubt distract from my lesson.

Mr. Fausett led us up the small hill in front of Astoria. Admiral ran between us, and we walked slowly while Sarah updated Mr. Fausett on the details of her wedding. I could recite her plans verbatim, as she had reviewed them so many times with me.

Mr. Dashel had a quaint home in London and a supposedly lovely estate in Suffolk. Sarah had told me I would be more than welcome after they completed their wedding trip and had some time to adjust as husband and wife. She did not need to say much more before I was convinced that the earliest I would see her new home was Christmas.

We had just neared the covering of yews when Admiral disappeared into the trees and began to bark. The behavior was so unlike his usual calm demeanor that I worried he may have been caught in a trap.

I ran ahead, following the sound of the commotion to the clearing I knew well. Charles and I had rambled and played fearlessly in these trees, and I knew each covey and burrow. At the edge of the glade, I heard a mumbled curse and realized it came from Mr. Brumley, who was lying on his back in the dirt.

Admiral bounded back towards me and playfully nipped at my skirts. Mr. Brumley noticed our presence, and the laugh that escaped my throat could not be helped. I tried to mute it with my hand, but upon Mr. Fausett questioning Charles, the humor I found in the scene became more than I could contain.

Mr. Brumley looked aghast, but before long the trace of a smile began to play at the corners of his mouth. He had looked so determined and serious last time I saw him. It was a welcome relief to see a smile light up his handsome face.

"Whatever are you doing on the ground, Brumley?" Mr. Fausett walked over to Charles's prostrate form.

"There's a certain dog that does not think I have a right to stand on my own two feet." He accepted Mr. Fausett's hand and stood.

Shock hit me as his words registered—Admiral had knocked him down. My laugh quickly died away. "Admiral? Mr. Brumley, am I to understand that Admiral is to blame for your . . . sitting in the dirt?"

Mr. Brumley stopped brushing the leaves from his coat and looked at me. "Yes, if I had *planned* to sit on the ground, I would have first laid down a blanket."

I took a step forward then stopped myself. "But he never acts out. He was trained to be a most proper and behaved companion." I could not account for it.

"Leah," Sarah placed a hand on my arm, "we mustn't forget that Admiral is an animal and subject to such behavior by the mere fact that he is a dog."

I shook my head. "It doesn't make sense."

"Perhaps it's simply me, Miss Leah. For this is the second time he has accosted me." Mr. Brumley bent over to retrieve a bow lying on the ground.

When Charles raised his head, our eyes met. He stared at me intently. The smile he'd dawned earlier was gone. His expression was not melancholy but rather one of expectation, a question, a yearning.

I blinked and recalled the topic we had been discussing—Admiral had assaulted Mr. Brumley before. "When was the first time Admiral accosted you?" I asked.

Charles took a measured breath and waited a moment before responding. "The accident with your father." He held my gaze.

"What?" Father's accident? What did Admiral have to do with Father getting shot? Charles had said it was him; he said it was his fault.

Sarah looked frantically between us then spoke. "Yes, Ferrin told me Admiral had jumped on you, Mr. Brumley."

The air felt suddenly heavy, and I struggled to draw a breath. "Ferrin most definitely did *not* tell me any such thing. He said nothing about

Admiral; in fact, very little was said on the matter." I turned to each of my companions. "Would someone please explain?" I raised my hands to my chest, hoping an explanation would ease the aching.

Charles ran a hand through his hair and huffed. "Very well." He walked slowly to a table stacked with arrows and set down the bow he held. Then he turned back towards me. "That morning," he took a settling breath, "Admiral began barking as the beaters drove the fowl to the air. I had shot one bird and was taking aim on a second. Then for some reason, Admiral jumped on me. The next thing I knew, I was flat on my back, and my gun had discharged." He returned his gaze to mine. "You know the rest, for you met us shortly after."

Oh!

"At the time, I had assumed he was excited about the sport. But—" Charles rubbed his hands over his eyes. "If I had only stopped to calm him . . ."

I *had* been there. I had run towards the rushes at the pond, precisely where the men were shooting. I had heard the barking and the shots— then the yelling.

Admiral was protecting me. The realization felt like getting dunked in a cold pond. Admiral had sensed my presence and tried to warn Charles— today and on the day of the hunt. Admiral knew I was nearby and in danger, and in warning he jumped on Charles.

It never was Charles's fault. I was to blame. Father's accident was my doing. It was entirely my fault. My legs felt detached, and the trees meshed into a fuzzy green fog. I was spinning and nauseated and heard enchanted voices floating around me.

"Leah?"

"Are you quite all right?"

"Catch her, Charles!" The last voice I recognized was Sarah's. Then I felt myself fall into a warm dream.

CHAPTER 43
Mr. Charles Brumley

❧

I HAD NEVER SEEN SOMEONE'S color drain as quickly as Leah's did in that moment. In Town, there was constant gossip about which debutante had suffered the most recent fit of vapors, but Miss Leah was made of heartier stuff. I had seen her color in her heightened fury. Never had I seen her faint.

Miss Hastings's voice pulled me out of my fear as Leah blanched. I caught her body as her legs collapsed beneath her. The moment turned frantic. Miss Hastings precipitously shook her sister's hand and called her name in an effort to wake her up.

I lifted Leah, placing one arm around her back and wrapping the other around her legs. Fausett ran ahead to request aid, and Miss Hastings skirted alongside while I carried Leah back to Astoria.

As I rushed towards the house, Leah's head jostled against my shoulder, and she moaned. I slowed my step and turned to see her eyes, brown and hazy, looking up at me.

"Charles," she said on a whisper.

"Hush, my dear." It hurt my heart to see her so indisposed. "We are almost to the house."

Leah nodded vaguely and leaned into my shoulder. She raised her arms and draped them around my neck. I pulled her closer and immediately felt her arms strengthen their hold.

I deposited her on the sofa in the drawing room and stepped back while Miss Hastings and Mrs. Clem took over the administrations.

"Come, Brumley." Fausett stepped next to me. "We should leave the ladies. Allow them some privacy." He exited, and after a long hesitation, I followed.

I did not want to leave. I wanted to make sure Leah was going to be all right. I had never seen her discomfited, and although she had already come to, I wanted to be there for her—and for me. To comfort her, to hold her, to have her call my name as if she actually needed me, wanted me. If only she longed for me as ardently as I ached for her.

I looked back again as I walked out the door. No part of Leah was visible, only the two women flittering over her. She was in capable hands, even though I wished they were mine.

"It would be best if we informed Mr. Hastings and Ferrin about Miss Leah's circumstance," Fausett said. "Then we may call tomorrow to check up on her."

"Deuced, Fausett! I'm not waiting until tomorrow to make sure she is well," I snapped at him and turned my attention from the drawing room.

Fausett had the audacity to look amused. "Very well. Let's first find her father."

CHAPTER 44
Miss Leah Hastings

❧❧❧

THERE WERE SEVERAL STRENGTHS I had always prided myself on. I could hold up my end in an engaging conversation. I was educated and well read to the point that I could converse on an infinite number of subjects. I was not a definitive beauty, but I was certainly not uncomely. I could ride reasonably well, and I could run fast, a fact to which Charles could attest. But I had never *ever* been a fragile female, wont to faint.

That I had succumbed to such a feminine stereotype did not sit well. Even worse was the revelation that had led to the unfortunate event. And while I did not feel myself in danger of fainting again, every time I recalled the reason for my sudden swoon, my heart sped.

Stupid girl! How had I been so blind? It was my nearness that had startled Admiral into a frenzy. I had acted on impulse, running towards the pond like I had. The rushes had hidden the men from my view, but Admiral had sensed it. I was heading back towards the house but had not made much progress when I heard the barking and the shots and then—

I shook my head clear of the image of Father's limp body being carried back to the house. As if on cue, to contradict the image in my mind, Father entered the room.

"Leah, my dear? What's this I hear about you fainting?" he asked.

I offered a meager smile.

"I thought you had resumed your regular walks. Your color had not quite returned, but you are not one to become easily tired or weary." He pulled a chair near the sofa where I lay.

"My sudden swoon," I rolled my eyes, "was not due to exhaustion, Father. It was due to a rather upsetting revelation."

At my words Sarah stopped bustling around and Aunt Evelyn leaned forward on her chair. It was not the ideal setting to share my confession, but I'd rather share it once than relay it to each of them individually.

Father sat, patiently waiting. I shifted to sit up, and Sarah moved to adjust several pillows around me while I steeled myself for the tempest that was about to hit. "Father, it was my fault you were shot."

And I told him all of it.

Sarah gasped, Aunt Evelyn made several covert comments, and Father sat stock-still. My admission was not met the way I had expected—although I wasn't really sure what I had anticipated.

When I knew of the circumstances surrounding Father's accident, I was livid. I couldn't fathom any explanation that could justify the error, the grave mistake that someone had made. Acknowledging that the fault was mine, entirely mine, should have elicited some sort of rebuke, some censure or reproof. Instead, Father was silent.

Both feet twitched in my boots, and I pinched my lips closed, waiting for Father to say something—anything. I was beyond desperate to get this over with.

Father's solemn eyes began to brighten. I turned my head and watched his transformation. He was not angry; instead he was . . . laughing? His smile spread to his eyes, and he released a hearty chuckle. His entire face lightened, and I could not understand it. My eyes narrowed, and confusion laced every line of my face. Why was he laughing?

"Oh, my dear." Father calmed himself and raised a hand to his injured shoulder. "Don't look so stern. It's not as bleak as all that."

Sarah appeared to be just as shocked as I was. Aunt Evelyn had pressed her lips into a hard line and said something under her breath.

Facing my father's smile, I asked, "Would you mind sharing what you find so humorous in this situation?" I could see nothing funny in my admission.

Father held up his hand and gave a dismissive wave. "I am sorry. Truly." He wiped his jaw and then placed his hands together in his lap.

"Aren't you angry?" I asked, my pulse elevating.

"No." Father shook his head, and his smile remained.

"But how? Why?" I cried, unable to understand the warring emotions of relief and guilt tumbling inside. "I should not have run towards the pond. I should have stayed clear of the hunt. If I had, none of this would have happened." I motioned to his shoulder.

"Leah," Father reached forward and took my hands in his, "do you recall the words of François de La Rochefoucauld?" My eyebrows pinched together in surprise, and Father continued. "*We forgive to the extent that we love*. I was never angry with Brumley, and I certainly hold you in higher regard than I do him."

"I don't understand. I deserve some sort of rebuke. It was so foolish of me," I said.

"My dear, there is a reason it is called an accident. I was not shot because of malice or spite. It was an accident and one which I am quite resigned to forget." Father's eyes twinkled, and he looked at me tenderly.

"You wish to forget? Put it behind as though it never happened?"

Father nodded.

"Me too." I smiled but quickly pushed it away. "There is one more person I must speak with." I took a deep breath. "Sarah, would you please ask Mr. Brumley to come in? It seems I owe him an apology." She left to find Charles, and I sighed. "Father, may I please speak with him alone?"

Father placed a hand on my shoulder and winked. "I believe we should retire to the library, Mrs. Clem." He stood, and Aunt Evelyn followed, clucking her tongue as she exited the room.

A minute later Charles stepped through the doorway, and I couldn't decide which was more difficult, forgiving or begging for forgiveness.

CHAPTER 45
Mr. Charles Brumley

❧

FAUSETT HAD BEEN CHASTISING ME for pacing the library carpet bare when Miss Hastings appeared. Her request was unexpected but entirely welcome. I stepped into the drawing room, where Miss Leah sat upright on the sofa.

"Miss Leah. Are you . . . recovered?" I asked.

Her pallor was still somewhat evident. She attempted to smile, but it was stilted and unsettled. She spoke as she examined her hands in her lap. "I am feeling much better." She looked quickly up through her lashes then returned her gaze to her fingers. "Thank you, Mr. Brumley, for your assistance."

The simple expression of gratitude brought a pink tinge to her cheeks. It bolstered my heart to see it.

"I'm sorry your efforts were in vain," Leah said. My confusion must have been obvious. "The archery," she clarified, looking up at me.

"'Tis nothing." I smiled. "The weather is not threatening, and Fausett and I determined we could leave the targets in place for a day or two."

Leah's lips curved slightly, but something was holding back her smile. I eyed her suspiciously.

"Won't you please have a seat, Mr. Brumley?" Leah asked. I glanced towards the door standing ajar, and Leah recognized my hesitation. "I told Father I wished to speak with you alone. He agreed, so I assure you it is quite all right for you sit down."

Slowly I lowered myself into a chair that had been moved near the sofa, intently watching Leah's face and wondering why she appeared so flustered. Her nerves must still be elevated from the episode in the trees.

Leah sighed deeply. "Charles." Her voice broke, pulling at my heartstrings.

She had used my Christian name. It was a rare enough occurrence that I knew something was wrong. I scanned her face, searching for a clue, for something, anything I could do to relieve some of the burden she felt. I leaned closer and opened my mouth to speak but closed it again as Leah shook her head.

"I'm so sorry," she whispered as tears trickled down her cheeks. My eyes scoured her face. My fingers twitched, and I could not resist wiping away her tears. Her eyes closed against my touch, and I leaned to the edge of my chair.

She shook her head and grabbed my hands in her own. She held them between us and opened her eyes, allowing new trails of tears to stream down her face. "It was my fault. All of it. Father's injury—I was there. Admiral knew, and he was trying to warn you." She choked on a sob. "I was so stupid! Why did I have to run?"

I felt helpless. "I don't understand." I freed one hand to pull the handkerchief from my pocket.

Leah released my fingers, accepted the linen, and swiped the tears from her red eyes. She gasped for a calming breath and inhaled deeply again. "The day Father was shot, I had run towards the pond. I didn't—I didn't think." She hung her head. "I heard the barking and realized my mistake, but it was too late. The shooting had begun, and Admiral jumped." Her tears ran freely as she returned her eyes to mine. "He was trying to protect me."

I rubbed my hands across my face, thinking through her words. Admiral had reacted the same way today. "You were there?" I asked, and Leah nodded. "And again today?" Another slight nod. It all became clear.

More tears slipped down her cheek. "Can you ever forgive me for being angry with you when the fault was entirely mine?"

I slipped my finger under her chin and raised her eyes to mine. "A woman I admire once told me I was forgiven. She said it had something to do with forgiving those we love." I wiped my thumb across her wet cheek.

She stiffened at my touch, and I began to pull my hand back. But she grabbed my fingers and laid them on her face. My heart erupted. Her soft skin felt like heaven. She held her hand over mine, and I stroked my thumb across her lips.

In a shaky whisper, she asked, "Does that mean you love me, Charles?"

My face split into a grin. "I'm afraid so."

A stifled laugh escaped. Her speckled eyes held me spellbound. "Are you really afraid to love me?"

She had to know. I needed her to know. I stood in front of the sofa and offered my free hand. She placed her shaky fingers in mine, and I lifted her to her feet. The blanket that had been draped over her fell to the floor. Both my arms slipped around her waist. "My darling Leah. I am only afraid that I don't deserve you." Leaning forward, I kissed her forehead. "But I will always love you." Then I bent my head and kissed her lips.

Her hands wrapped around my neck and tangled in my hair. I held her as close as I dared, pulling her near and relishing the soft, gentle movement of our lips. It was a kiss eleven years in the making, and we thoroughly made up for each of those years.

We separated, and I gave Leah a final tender kiss on the side of her mouth, but I did not let her go. Instead, I pulled her close. She rested her head upon my shoulder.

And that is how Mr. Hastings found us when he reentered the room. "Ahem." He cleared his throat. "Brumley, may I have a word?"

Leah smiled and did not attempt to conceal the color that had returned rather forcefully to her cheeks. She excused herself, proclaiming that she felt miraculously better and would like to enjoy the fresh air of the garden.

Mr. Hastings and I were left alone, and he began to relate a very interesting tale about a particularly presumptuous mother.

"So you're telling me the old bat was behind it all along?" I asked, pushing up from my seat.

He chuckled. "Now, now. I'll deal with Mrs. Ansley. Remember her heart is cold because it has never been touched with love. She has no notion of the endearment."

"You are a true gentleman indeed to be able to forgive her so quickly," I said.

"We all need forgiveness, Brumley. The good Lord knew that from the beginning. I just as soon be ahead in the game. My turn for penance will come soon enough, as will yours."

He was absolutely correct, and I nodded my agreement. "And what of Captain Wilkins?" I asked.

"Ah, yes, the captain. The one you fetched to Landers Lodge." Mr. Hastings raised his brows.

"I suppose that was rather brash," I admitted.

"You are a good man. You know Leah well enough to love her in spite of her faults."

His reference to my love for his daughter left me feeling exposed, and I shifted awkwardly, unable to formulate a response.

He laughed again then stood and shook my hand. "I've always liked you, Brumley."

"Thank you, sir. I assure you the feeling is mutual."

"I advise you to properly court my daughter before you attempt to kiss her like that again."

I cleared my throat. "Yes, sir."

He released his grip. "Now, I believe you will find Leah in the garden. Go." He shooed me towards the door.

I felt like a giddy schoolboy with this turn of events. Last night I did not think it possible. Now I jogged through the garden paths, circling and searching, desperate for a sight of her.

There.

She was tilting her head back and holding her face to the sun. Her eyes were closed, and her hands were clasped behind her. My steps quieted as I closed the distance, taking in every part of her. Peaceful and serene. I stopped a yard away, and she must have felt my gaze for her eyes popped open wide.

"Do you mean to frighten me, Mr. Brumley?" she asked, looking up through her lashes with a demure smile and crimson checks.

"Frighten you, no. Admire you, yes." I grinned and took another step closer as she rolled her eyes. "I have spoken with your father."

Her blush deepened. "Oh?" Her breath seemed to catch.

"He told me the whole of it." I shook my head and took another step towards her. "I wish I would have known."

"I am forgiven?" she asked.

"Hmmm." I crossed my arms and leaned back, rubbing my chin as if pondering some great thought. "I'll consider it."

"Charles Christopher Brumley!" she said sternly.

I stepped forward and reached for her fingers, lifting them between us. "Of course you are forgiven, dear Leah. These past months have been torture, the coldest of winters. After the accident, I thought there was no way you could love me."

"Why didn't you tell me about Admiral?" Her eyes turned sad. "Did you have so little faith in me that you thought I could not forgive?"

"No, my darling. I had so little faith in myself." I pulled her nearer. "I saw all of my weaknesses, all of my flaws." A rogue curl blew across her face, and I could not help but brush it away. "I should have tried sooner, and I regret the days lost to my foolish insecurities."

Leah pulled back slightly. "And then you showed up with Captain Wilkins!"

I groaned. "I held no hope for my own happiness, and I only thought of you. I fetched the captain because I wanted you to be happy. I did not realize how it would tear me apart." I studied her face, and her speckled eyes searched mine. Somewhere between us an understanding passed. It was the same understanding we'd had as children. Our opinions may vary or our words collide, but our hearts would not, could not, be separated by such petty folly. We would always return to the same place, and that was here, hand in hand, so blissful with one another that all mistakes were forgiven.

"Your absence from my life was devastating," I whispered.

Leah smiled. "You know I am not entirely to blame. It was you who left first, Charles. And I would very much like to know why." She looked down, staring at her hands in mine.

"You misunderstand." I reached my hand up to her cheek, and she closed her eyes and leaned into my palm. "I've been devastated these past six years. Ever since our carriage whisked me off to Cambridge."

Her eyes flew open, and a faint smile traced her lips. I leaned forward and placed a single kiss on those soft lips. She felt perfect there in my arms, and I never wanted to be without her.

I inhaled the scent of lavender and pressed my cheek into her abundant curls as she said, "I believe now I can begin to feel whole once more."

CHAPTER 46
Mrs. Leah Hastings

ᘓᕒ᪥ᕑᘓ

CHARLES TOLD ME EVERYTHING. FROM the moment he knew he loved me to the moment of Father's accident. I filled in my own story, meeting Captain Wilkins and what I had interpreted Charles's indifference to mean.

We could now laugh at our folly, but we both agreed that our misunderstandings, our misinterpretations had led us to this point—the point of being blessedly happy with one another. I loved Charles and he loved me, and while we still disagreed on various topics, we would always end our disputes with an embrace or a gentle kiss. Persuasion was not such a bad thing.

We were married in the last remains of summer. It was very much like that day at the river when Charles had teased me, dared me, and charmed me. Now, however, the teasing was endearing, the dares had subsided, and the charming I welcomed and tried to reciprocate.

Admiral died eight months later. His jubilant personality had slowly faded as he slipped away. Charles and I buried him in the glen in the forest. I stood in the clearing as Charles tipped the last shovelful of dirt on the small grave. I knelt and placed a bouquet of forget-me-nots on the freshly turned earth.

"He was a faithful companion," Charles said.

"And a fierce guardian," I added.

"May Admiral rest in peace."

"Amen."

Charles had collected a large round rock from the riverbed, and he now placed it as a tribute to Admiral at the head of the grave.

We stood in silence with Charles's arms wrapped firmly around me. The peace I had yearned for flowed between us and held us together. I looked towards the sky, picking out a sliver of blue through the trees. I inhaled deeply and turned my eyes to my husband. "Shall we head back?" I asked.

He smiled his consent.

We walked arm in arm toward the house, quietly beaming in the happiness of life. When we stepped out from the trees, a mischievous grin split my face.

Charles looked at me curiously as I slipped my arm from his.

"Leah?" he asked with apprehension and turned sideways towards me.

The opportunity he presented was too ideal. "First one to the gardens picks the stakes!" I yelled. Then I turned and ran down the hill while Charles laughed behind me.

He won, and I was perfectly content with the outcome of our wager. Charles chose a kiss as his stakes, and I was more than willing to comply. After all, he won by quite a lot.

ABOUT THE AUTHOR

Photo courtesy of Gary Underwood

CHALON LINTON WAS FIRST INTRODUCED to the Regency era by a dear friend, and now she can't get enough of handsome men in tailcoats. Chalon's intrigue in the genre stems from a nostalgic longing for manners, wit, and true love. Fortunately, she found her dashing gentleman, married him, and now lives happily ever after in Southern California.